Short Cuts

Children's Books by
Sigmund Brouwer

FROM BETHANY HOUSE PUBLISHERS

THE ACCIDENTAL DETECTIVES

The Volcano of Doom
The Disappearing Jewel of Madagascar
Legend of the Gilded Saber
Tyrant of the Badlands
Shroud of the Lion
Creature of the Mists
The Mystery Tribe of Camp Blackeagle
Madness at Moonshiner's Bay
Race for the Park Street Treasure
Terror on Kamikaze Run
Lost Beneath Manhattan
The Missing Map of Pirate's Haven
The Downtown Desperadoes
Sunrise at the Mayan Temple
Phantom Outlaw at Wolf Creek
Short Cuts

WATCH OUT FOR JOEL!

Bad Bug Blues
Long Shot
Camp Craziness
Fly Trap
Mystery Pennies
Strunk Soup

www.coolreading.com

05A

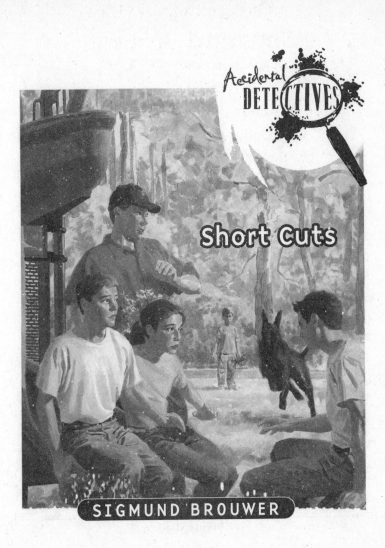

Accidental DETECTIVES

Short Cuts

SIGMUND BROUWER

BETHANYHOUSE
MINNEAPOLIS, MINNESOTA

Published by Bethany House Publishers
11400 Hampshire Avenue South
Bloomington, Minnesota 55438

Bethany House Publishers is a division of
Baker Publishing Group, Grand Rapids, Michigan.

Printed in the United States of America

Library of Congress Cataloging-in-Publication Data

Brouwer, Sigmund, 1959-
    Short cuts / by Sigmund Brouwer.
       p. cm. — (Accidental detectives)
    Summary: A collection of stories featuring twelve-year-old Ricky Kidd and some of the lessons he has learned about life.
    ISBN 0-7642-2579-0 (pbk.)
    [1. Christian life—Fiction. 2. Conduct of life—Fiction.] I. Title: Shortcuts.
II. Title III. Series: Brouwer, Sigmund, ,d 1959- Accidental detectives.
    PZ7.B789984Sh   2005
    [Fic]—dc22

                                                        2004020613

SIGMUND BROUWER is the award-winning author of scores of books. He speaks to kids around the continent in an effort to instill good reading and writing habits in the next generation. Sigmund and his wife, Cindy Morgan, divide their time between Tennessee and Alberta, Canada.

For Olivia
and the sunshine you bring
into this world

CONTENTS

Introduction.. 11

1 Crazy As Foxes 21
   Daredevils: Thoughts on *Crazy As Foxes*

2 The Banker Down the Street 33
   The Greatest Gift: Thoughts on *The Banker Down the Street*

3 Celestial C. Moondust................................. 45
   Is God Real? Thoughts on *Celestial C. Moondust*

4 Magic Pennies 57
   Pangs of the Heart: Thoughts on *Magic Pennies*

5 Old Friends 65
   Who Will You Be? Thoughts on *Old Friends*

6 The Hero of Jamesville............................... 77
   "Nyah, nyah, nenyahnyah": Thoughts on *The Hero of Jamesville*

7 Current Events... 87
   Contents—One World/Handle With Care: Thoughts on
       Current Events

8 The Fight 99
   Swing, Duck, or Run Away: Thoughts on *The Fight*

9 The Baseball Feud 111
   The Ache to Belong: Thoughts on *The Baseball Feud*

10 Blindsided 121
    The Trouble of Life: Thoughts on *Blindsided*

11 Crazy Carl 131
    Freedom of the Spirit: Thoughts on *Crazy Carl*

INTRODUCTION

My name is Ricky Kidd. I'm not fond of homework. But when my teacher told me this week's assignment was to write a report on an author, I figured life could be worse.

You see, I've had dreams of being a writer myself. My mother always accuses me of having a hyperactive imagination, and I've been involved in one or two crazy adventures in my life, so maybe someday I'll have the chance to write about them.

Anyway, I had to do this author report, and my teacher assigned me someone named *Sigmund Brouwer* as my subject.

Sigmund Brouwer? The name sounded strangely familiar, but I told myself not to jump to conclusions, at least not until I knew more about him.

I should get an A+ on my assignment, just for the effort I put into research. I even wrote a letter to Mr. Brouwer to find out how old he is, where he lives, when he began to write, and stuff like that.

He did write back, and what I discovered—I'm sad to report—is not impressive.

Sigmund Brouwer is nearly ninety years old. From birth he has drooled constantly, so much so that hired help must follow him around with buckets and mops to make sure nobody slips in the puddles he leaves behind.

Not only that, but Sigmund Brouwer—

TIME OUT! WHOOAA! STOP! DO NOT LISTEN TO RICKY KIDD! It's me here. Sigmund Brouwer.

My editor and I thought it might be a good idea for me to write an introduction to this book. For a few reasons, that idea made me nervous. In fact, as you'll discover, following each short story are some of my thoughts and the background of that story. Writing those parts also made me nervous.

So it dawned on me that since I let Ricky do all the talking in all the ACCIDENTAL DETECTIVES books, maybe he should do the introduction for this book, too. *Sure,* I thought, *he can give a bit of my background; then I can pretend he wrote a letter to me, and I'll reply with what I need to say and have Ricky faithfully pass that letter on to you.*

It might have worked, too, until the little rat started to lie.

No, I am *not* ninety years old. I have not drooled since birth. Sure, I might get a runny nose whenever I have a cold, but certainly not enough to pay anyone to mop up after me.

My hunch is Ricky Kidd was using that outrageous lie to tell me that the introduction was not *his* job, but *mine*, and if I was going to dump it on him, he'd do his best to make me regret it.

Obviously, I would and did.

Which means I can't hide behind him for this introduction. Which means I'll have to officially start now. And if that's the case, I'd like to explain why I was nervous about this introduction and parts of this book.

It's for the very reason that I can't hide behind Ricky Kidd from the first to the last page as I've done with the other—fifteen so far—mysteries of the ACCIDENTAL DETECTIVES.

If you have read any of the ACCIDENTAL DETECTIVES books before, you know that Ricky Kidd is the one who tells you the story as it unravels, the one who faints whenever his younger brother,

Joel, suddenly appears, the one who blushes when Lisa Higgins gives him a kiss on the cheek, the one who hates trouble but gets dragged into it by his friends.

As a writer it's fun to hide behind Ricky Kidd. See, it goes back to the HARDY BOYS mysteries. By age twelve I had read all fifty mysteries—there are way, way more now—most of them three or four times each. Even today—more than thirty years after reading one—I can picture Frank and Joe Hardy and their friends solving mysteries all over Canada and the United States.

At age twelve I used to daydream for hours about how I'd help Frank and Joe solve a mystery if they ever got in trouble anywhere near my school. Yup, maybe I'd untie them just before the train ran them over, and then together we'd rescue the three beautiful women who were about to be pushed off the cliff. (Actually, two beautiful women and one beautiful twelve-year-old girl, because if Frank and Joe were going to get adoring sighs and maybe grateful kisses from the women, I sure didn't want to get left out on any of that stuff—though I was more interested in someone my own age!)

And now I can hardly believe I'm able to have all these adventures with Ricky Kidd. If you'd have told the twelve-year-old me that someday he'd be able to take all his daydreams about mysteries and adventures and make them happen in books, the kid would have been delirious with excitement. But now he's me, and together it's happening, and the twelve-year-old in me gives me high fives whenever I think about how great all of this is. (Does that make sense?)

The other thing about hiding behind Ricky Kidd is that it is safer behind him. Or at least safer pretending everything said is what *he* says. That way if things go wrong, it's not my fault, right?

In this book, though, Ricky Kidd does step aside after each short story, and I do some talking for myself. I'm nervous that some people will think I'm offering my thoughts and opinions as if those thoughts and opinions are absolutely right and true and there is no other way of looking at things. I'd be embarrassed if people got that impression.

For starters, it would be terribly presumptuous on my part. There *are* some "absolute truths," things that no one can or should deny, but whatever is absolutely right and true doesn't need anyone's help, let alone mine. If something is right and true, it will stand for itself under any questions for any length of time, regardless of whatever puny words I might try to add to those truths.

But in areas of opinion, who am I to say that my opinions are right and yours are wrong, especially without listening to another viewpoint?

I hope, then, you realize that I just want to start or encourage whatever questions you might have on the subject of the related short story. If I manage to give you another perspective that helps as you're thinking about these issues—great!

Of course, much of a person's understanding of life grows out of his or her background. If you were raised on a Montana ranch, you would probably see and deal with some situations much differently than someone raised in the east end of Los Angeles.

That's why, as you might remember, at the beginning of this introduction I was going to have Ricky Kidd mention some of my own background in his school report. Then you would know where I was coming from.

And I'd still like to get Ricky involved in all of this. He shouldn't be able to get away as easily as he thinks.

What should I do? Hmm. Maybe he'll have to interview me. That way, we're *both* responsible....

Ricky Kidd: If I'm back, I guess it means I still have to do the report, huh. Unfortunately, I hear my friend Mike Andrews calling. He wants to play some street hockey.

S.B.: I've got it on good authority that you might be going to Colorado soon. [Editor's note: Indeed, one of the ACCIDENTAL DETECTIVES mysteries is set in Colorado.] If I put in the word, that trip can be canceled. Interested in Colorado during your next Christmas vacation? At a ski resort that was built overtop an abandoned gold mine somewhere in the glorious Rocky Mountains and—

Ricky Kidd: Mike and street hockey can wait, sir. I'll just dig out my notebook and pen.

S.B.: That's what I thought.

Ricky Kidd: Hmmm. First question, then. Where were you born?

S.B.: In a hospital.

Ricky Kidd: Good one, sir.

S.B.: And you think I was happy with those cracks about being a ninety-year-old drooler? All right, I was born in Red Deer, Alberta, Canada. In 1959.

Ricky Kidd: That still makes you pretty old, doesn't it?

S.B.: Next question, please.

Ricky Kidd: Born and raised there?

S.B.: I left Red Deer when I was eighteen to go to Calvin College in Grand Rapids, Michigan. I graduated with a bachelor's degree in economics, then traveled and worked some, then went to Carleton University in Ottawa, Ontario, Canada, where I took journalism, actually graduated, then worked in Florida before moving back home. I missed Red Deer a lot. Family and people there, beauty of the countryside . . . it only took about nine years of travel to discover that the grass was greener on my side of the fence, back home in Alberta.

Ricky Kidd: Alberta—that's north of Montana, right?

S.B.: You bet. It's a province about the size of Texas. We've got mountains to the west and prairie to the east, great unexplored wilderness to the north and even our own semi-desert badlands. Red Deer itself has grown to about seventy thousand people, not like when I was a kid when the population was barely twenty-five thousand—

Ricky Kidd: Wouldn't a person have to be old to see his hometown more than double in size?

S.B: I really should cancel your next adventure.

Ricky Kidd: Sorry.

S.B.: What was I saying?

Ricky Kidd: Something about the city doubling in size.

S.B.: Right. We had an oil boom in the 1970s that caused things to grow fast. But I always remember Red Deer as a nice small town, similar to your town of Jamesville. It's beautiful in Red Deer. Set in a valley. A river running through it. On a clear day you can see the Rocky Mountains to the west. Between us and the mountains, there are rolling hills of wheat and pasture, lots of lakes, forests, great fishing streams, and—

Ricky Kidd: Sir, my teacher would get mad at me if I gave her a travel brochure instead of an author report.

S.B.: Sorry.

Ricky Kidd: How long have you been writing stories?

S.B.: Unofficially since the fourth grade. But it wasn't until I was twenty that I *officially* thought I would do it.

Ricky Kidd: Officially?

S.B.: You know how it is at younger ages. One day you want to be a firefighter when you grow up, the next a doctor. When I was twenty—even though you'd be stretching it to call me grown-up then—I decided I wanted to be a writer.

Ricky Kidd: So you officially became a writer at age twenty.

S.B.: No.

Ricky Kidd: But you said—

S.B.: I officially *wanted* to become a writer at that age. It took nearly seven years before anything I wrote was published in a magazine. That was a short story. It's probably safer to say I officially *became* a writer then. After that came more published short stories until a few years later I happened to write a couple of mysteries which involved—um—someone a lot like you.

Ricky Kidd: Oh.

S.B.: I think it was what I learned from sports that really helped as I tried to first get published.

Ricky Kidd: Sports and writing. This ought to be good.

S.B.: Remember Colorado when you try that kind of sarcasm on me—

Ricky Kidd: You had mentioned sports and writing, sir?

S.B.: I really wanted to be a good hockey player when I was growing up. You know, dreams about the big leagues. Obviously, I didn't make it. I played on my college team and even briefly for a bush-league semi-pro team in Michigan; however, I knew long before I was twenty that nobody would be begging me to sign a contract to play professionally. But I did learn something very crucial.

Ricky Kidd: How to duck? I mean, it looks like you have all your teeth, and I've heard—

S.B.: Actually, my front two teeth are gone, thanks to a misunderstanding with a hockey stick. They're capped now. What I learned was the same thing I later learned from racquetball. Whatever you dream—sports, music, arts, medicine—you won't reach it without two secrets.

Ricky Kidd: Talent is one of them, right?

S.B.: Talent probably helps, but it isn't *needed*. There was a player, Spud Webb, in the National Basketball League who was at least a foot—more often nearly two feet—shorter than most of his opponents. I wouldn't say he was naturally built for his sport. But he was still there. I'd guess he applied those two simple secrets.

Ricky Kidd: I give up. What are the two secrets?

S.B.: Practice. And never quit.

Ricky Kidd: That's it? I thought writing took creativity, imagination. All that stuff.

S.B.: All the creativity and imagination won't do you any good unless you learn to put words together. Practice. And never quit. Writing is like sports. Hit ten thousand slapshots in hockey, and you can't help but have a better slapshot. Write a couple thousand pages, and you'll improve. Guaranteed.

Ricky Kidd: You said it took nearly seven years to get published. Is that what you mean by "never quit"?

S.B.: I, uh, was too dumb to quit. I mean, I thought everything I wrote was good enough to get published next week. If I had been smart enough to know it was so bad that the "next week" was going to take seven years, it would have been tougher to continue.

Ricky Kidd: I'll remember that, because I've had some really crazy adventures. Almost like mysteries. A couple in New York. One in Florida where I was nearly eaten by an alligator. Pirates' treasure in San Diego. A phantom outlaw in Montana. Stuff like that. Someday I'd like to write about them.

S.B.: Mayan legends in Mexico? A lake monster in Canada?

Ricky Kidd: That's uncanny! I've had adventures both those places, too! It's like you can read my mind!

S.B.: I don't know how to break this to you, especially if you want to use those mysteries in your own writing career—

Ricky Kidd: Yes?

S.B.: Well—no, I'd rather not break it to you. Let's talk about that another time, okay? Um, don't you need more material for your report? My family background, maybe.

Ricky Kidd: Are you changing the subject?

S.B.: I thought the subject was *me.* I have four sisters and a brother. I'm the oldest of us six kids. I was also the most perfect. People used to travel for hundreds of miles just to see me so they would know what a perfect child looked like, especially one who could remain so saintly when the four sisters and brother were so terrible. To this day I insist it was not I who put the snakes in the bathtub before my mother took the shower that sent her to the hospital. No way. It was my brother, Robert. Now, I admit it seems odd, because he was only six months old at the time and stuck in a playpen, but that little squirt could come and go like a little ghost, even then. He must have slipped through the bars—are you hearing this, Mom?—and somehow stolen the very snakes that I had found only minutes earlier, then—

Ricky Kidd: I have a brother like that: Joel.

S.B.: You actually believe me?

Ricky Kidd: I think you have a tendency to exaggerate, sir. I'll be putting that in my report.

S.B.: I think you should put your notebook away instead. Why don't you, uh, tell me about your friends.

Ricky Kidd: Changing the subject again, sir?

S.B.: I said, tell me about your friends. You know, *the ones who might be in Colorado* with you soon?

Ricky Kidd: *Those* friends. We'd hate to miss Colorado, sir. There's Mike Andrews. He's got red hair and freckles. *Trouble* is his middle name; he thinks the word *impossible* just means try harder. Then there's Ralphy Zee. Skinny, brown hair, computer genius type who's not eager to go into dark alleys. Also Lisa Higgins. Strong and smarter than the guys, drives us nuts, but also pretty with dark hair and a smile—

S.B.: You're blushing. Sure she's not a little more than a friend?

Ricky Kidd: And, of course, Joel. Quiet, always follows me around, pops up from nowhere at the worst times. His only weak point is a stupid teddy bear that he carries everywhere. And I have a new baby sister named Rachel. She's very sweet. Sometimes I try to sing songs to her when nobody is around to listen, but usually it makes her cry because I'm so bad at singing and—

S.B.: I'm not the only one good at changing the subject.

Ricky Kidd: Sir?

S.B.: Forget it. Um, sounds like you have interesting friends.

Ricky Kidd: They're great. It seems like something is always happening when they're around. Some days I think I should write stories about them.

S.B.: Funny you should mention that. . . .

CRAZY AS FOXES 1

I knew I was in trouble when the rain got so hard and gray that I couldn't see the front end of the canoe. That normally wouldn't have made me nervous, except not only was I already sitting in the front of the canoe, but it had been half an hour since we last saw shore.

I didn't bother asking myself how I ever managed to be in such a situation. For one thing, the waves were pounding so hard the answer would be tough to hear. For another thing, I didn't want to look like a chicken. And third, I knew the answer anyway.

Only one person in the world gets me doing things I'd never in a million years do by myself. And he was in the back of the canoe, bailing water more than he was paddling. It makes you wonder how someone like that can be your best friend for so many years.

Trouble was spelled M-I-K-E; it was Mike Andrews' fault we were in the middle of a lake, trying to survive a sudden and vicious thunderstorm.

Earlier we had been paddling near the shore, and Mike had said, "Let's head for the other side. First one to turn around loses."

"You're nuts," I'd said. "It's ten miles away."

Our parents had dropped us off with a few of our

friends for the day. We had life jackets, and, because they'd spent lots of time teaching us, we knew how to handle canoes, so they weren't worried.

They should have been.

Because Mike had said, "I guess anybody but a wimp could help me paddle to the other side and back in only a few hours."

"Mike—" but I knew pleading would have been useless. I gritted my teeth. Who was he to think I would turn around first?

"Okay," I said. "I bet you chicken out first."

"Not a chance, pal. In fact, let's say that the first one to chicken out owes the other guy a movie with popcorn."

"Hah!"

The journey was on.

It took only until land was out of sight for the rain to begin coming down like bullets.

"Mike," I shouted. "Don't you think we should turn around?"

"Hah, hah!" he laughed crazily into the teeth of the rain. "Are you chicken?"

For once I nearly said yes. Maybe, if we were lucky, we could get back to shore before tipping or filling up with water.

Instead, I acted cool, which can be hard to do with a lot of water running down your back.

"Only nerds are chicken," I shouted. "And I thought maybe you were getting scared already."

"Hah, hah! *I'm* not going to be the one to turn back. Unless you want to say uncle and lose the bet!"

"Not me!" I yelled and nearly choked on the wave that hit the front of the canoe and threw water into my face. "We both know you'll give up first."

He didn't say anything because I ducked the next wave and it got him right between the eyes. The rain and wind only got worse, and both of us kept paddling for the far shore, miles away. I tried not to think about the worst that could happen as my arms got more and more tired and my skin got more and more cold.

Out there in the lake, fighting the winds and waves, my brother, Joel, should have been the last thing on my mind. But right then I envied him, somewhere back on land, probably in the campground shelter waiting out the rain.

And I remembered something else about Joel.

Once, in a restaurant, Mom said she was proud of him because he never cared about other people's opinions.

Can you figure? There I was with the rain stinging my face so hard I couldn't even tell if I was crying, and I could only picture Joel praying before the meal in a restaurant. He had solemnly folded his hands and prayed out loud the longest and slowest blessing on the food that you could imagine.

In fact, prayer is about the only time Joel really talks. And this prayer went on and on. I was getting embarrassed, especially because Joel's teddy bear was propped on the table in front of us. I was looking away so people around us wouldn't think he was *my* brother, and Mom stopped me with sad eyes.

"Ricky," she had said when he finally finished, "promise me you won't fall into the trap of doing things simply to make other people happy."

At the time I'd thought she meant saying no to drugs and smoking and stuff, but now I realized she'd been talking about even more than that.

And I wondered exactly who I was making happy by continuing to paddle for the far shore. Especially if it might kill me.

"Mike!" I shouted. "I quit! You win! Let's turn around!"

"What?" he shouted back.

"Uncle! Auntie! Nephew! I give up. Let's go back!"

"Too late!" he shouted. "We must be halfway there already! It's shorter to keep going!"

What was he? Nuts? We couldn't possibly be halfway there! He was going to kill us!

"No! No! No!" I yelled and ducked another wave. "That's impossible! Turn us around!"

"Keep paddling!" he shouted.

We were in big trouble. Mike was in the back, and in a canoe, that's the place for steering. There was nothing I could do in the front to turn us around. And the rain got worse.

"Please, Mike!" I tried again. "Turn us around before it's too late! I'm scared!"

"Keep paddling!" he shouted.

It was the only thing to do besides pray. Which I did, too. I prayed and I paddled until my arms fell off, then paddled some more because if we stopped . . .

Suddenly I fell forward in the canoe and landed in the water! I didn't even have time to shout. Then I banged my nose into gravel. We had hit land, but it was raining so hard we couldn't even see it. I stood up and shouted with joy!

Mike jumped out of the canoe and hauled it onto the beach. Then we ran under some trees and lay there panting. I decided even being wet and cold was fantastic as long as it wasn't being wet and cold out in the middle of the lake.

When we could both breathe again, I turned to Mike.

"You were right," I said. "We *were* closer to the other shore. I owe you a movie for chickening out, but I'm so glad to be here I don't even care. Thanks for saving our lives by not listening to me and turning around."

He shrugged. "No problem."

That's when I noticed a pair of little legs coming out from behind a tree.

"Aaack!" I nearly fainted. Then I relaxed. It was Joel. Naturally, he was wearing a jacket and didn't look cold at all.

"Did you catch fish?" he asked.

"No," I snapped. "We didn't catch any fish. We were lucky to—"

I stopped. Joel? Joel? We weren't on the far shore? And Mike had been in the back, steering the canoe the whole time out there?

Mike must have known what I was thinking. He stood.

"What am I, crazy?" he said. "If you were steering in the back of the canoe, wouldn't you turn around in a storm like that? But slow enough so that someone else in the front might not notice?"

He saw the look in my eyes and started running.

"And by the way!" he shouted over his shoulder. "Don't worry about buying me a movie!"

By that time my feet were pounding the ground harder than the rain, and Mike was lucky to be staying just out of reach.

DAREDEVILS:
Thoughts on *Crazy As Foxes*

WHEN I WAS FOURTEEN, I jumped off a bridge.

I'd like to blame it on Cousin Jeff. (Jeff is not his real name, but since what follows has never been made public, I'd prefer to protect both of us.)

Cousin Jeff lived in the valley of our town of Red Deer, a block away from the wide river that runs through town. Once or twice a week that summer I'd pedal across town and we'd find things to do.

There was the day we flushed a gopher—ground squirrel—from its burrow by dumping enough buckets of water into the hole so that the gopher finally emerged, gasping for air and slick with mud.

We had great plans for that gopher. Rodeo plans. If you've ever seen the calf-tying event at a rodeo, you would know what I mean. The cowboys "hog-tie" the calf, using a short piece of rope to cinch the back legs to the front legs.

That was the plan for our gopher. Jeff had grabbed it by the scruff of the neck, and my job was to use a shoelace to tie its legs together. What we'd do next never even crossed our minds. I think the point was to see if it could be done.

It didn't get done.

Our thoughtless cruelty was amply and immediately repaid. Cousin Jeff lost his nerve and let go of the now-angry gopher, which in turn snapped its head forward and bit my right forefinger hard enough that its teeth met somewhere in the middle, hard enough that it took five seconds of yelling and jumping to shake it loose. A tiny, jagged white scar still remains as a reminder that rodeo events should be left to cowboys, not to Cousin Jeff and me—the sucker doing the dirty work.

I should have learned then.

But I didn't.

After that, because of Cousin Jeff, I once found myself fleeing through an old lady's yard a half block over. Seconds later an invisible hand slammed me backward into the ground.

I'd been clotheslined. Literally.

The old lady had a clothesline stretched across her yard, and on this day no blankets, shirts, or pants were pinned to dry, so there was no fair indication of the line's existence. Instead, bare of any clothing, and against the background of dark green trees, the steel wire of the clothesline was almost invisible. Cousin Jeff knew about it; he'd ripped through this yard dozens of times, and he ducked in time. Not me. The line caught me across the mouth as I hit it at full tilt, leaving me as stunned and bewildered as any bird that has flown unaware into a clear glass window.

End result?

A throbbing head from where I'd slammed the ground. Deep cuts across both sides of my mouth. A chipped tooth. And Cousin Jeff doubled over in laughter.

I didn't learn then.

Because on my next visit, Cousin Jeff told me about a pipe that ran along the underside of the bridge, just upstream.

"Hey," he said, swaggering, "we cross the bridge on that pipe all the time. The edge of the girders gives you a foothold, and you grab the pipe with both arms and slide forward."

"Across the entire river?" I could not believe him.

"Yeah. What else?"

I tried to picture the bridge. It spanned three, maybe four huge concrete pilings. From the top of the pilings, it seemed maybe a three-story drop to the water.

"Aren't you afraid of falling?" I asked.

His look turned to scorn. "If you don't want to...."

That look said enough.

What I haven't explained is that I was the kind of kid who mostly read books. It was bad enough to be labeled a brain because I did grades three and four in one year. But I read books. And I had a mother who didn't like any of her children to do things that made their clothes dirty, and who believed in putting disinfectant and Band-Aids on the smallest of cuts. I wasn't tall then, either. (Just after high school, I grew six inches to put me over the six-foot mark, but until then I was always one of the smallest guys in the class—every class from grade four to twelve.)

Another way of putting it is this: Does the word *nerd* ring a bell?

Cousin Jeff, however, was a year older, and tough. Nobody I knew messed with him. He'd always been tough, too. Once, when he was six and I was five, he cut his finger. Six-year-olds usually get upset over stuff like that. Not Cousin Jeff. Even then he was too cool to show pain. He just sucked the blood until most of the bleeding had stopped, then wiped the rest on his shirt. His actions were enough of a symbol of disregard for the way mothers ruled the world that I remained deeply impressed with him for years.

This summer was special, then: Cousin Jeff was allowing me into his rough-and-tumble world. To remain there—and in his good graces—I simply had to measure up to it with no complaints, shrug off the pain of a gopher bite that should have been stitched, smile through the blood in my mouth from clotheslining myself, and accept any challenge.

So when Cousin Jeff gave me that look of scorn, I had no choice.

"Bridge-crossing," I said. "No problem."

"Actually, we don't cross the entire bridge."

"Whatever," I said with coolness. I wasn't going to let him see my relief.

"Yeah, we only go to the second-to-last piling," he said. "Then we jump."

"Oh."

Cousin Jeff hadn't lied about the pipe. It was thick enough that I couldn't wrap my arms around it. Spaced brackets held it suspended a few feet away from the girders of the underside of the bridge. Using the pipe for support, then, meant leaning across that open space, with the river below. Above us, the structure rumbled with crossing cars—drivers and passengers unaware of our plans.

Cousin Jeff looked back, grinned, then began to shuffle and balance a slow forward progress.

I followed.

Each second was an agony of slowness. *If my arms slip* . . . There were gravel bars, rough and jagged above the shallow parts of the river. *Surely he isn't serious about the jumping part. . . .*

I have no idea how long it took to reach the second-to-last support piling. I do remember casting fond glances at the last piling and the safety of the other shore just beyond.

But Cousin Jeff stopped and, in one smooth motion, pushed from the pipeline, off the edge girder, and onto the wide, flat surface of that second-to-last piling.

I followed.

We could stand there without stooping. The road of the bridge rumbled directly above our heads. Far below, the current of the river swirled and snarled around the base of the piling.

"You've jumped from here?" I hoped that Cousin Jeff missed the falter in my voice.

"All the time."

"Oh."

We stared downward and watched the dark water with the same devoted fascination given to the flames of campfires.

"Here?"

He nodded.

"Jump?"

He kept nodding.

"Down?"

"Yup."

We stared more. But I knew that the longer I thought about it, the more afraid I would be.

"Okay," I said.

And I jumped.

The swirling water rushed at me at about a million miles an hour, but it still took forever to slam into the river. I went under, but I failed to keep from going too far down, and before I could recover, the water had swept me downstream a bus length or two; then I fought my way to shallow water where I could stand waist deep and lean against the current.

Cousin Jeff was still on the piling.

"Hey!" I shouted in his direction, happy to have survived.

"Have you lost your mind?" he yelled back. "You jumped!"

"Yeah!" I shouted back. "Hurry. This water's getting cold!"

Even as far from him as I was, I could see the stunned disbelief on his face.

It began to dawn on me that he had no intention of jumping.

I scrambled and waded to shore, marched over to the bridge—dripping wet, of course—climbed the short, steep embankment, reached the girder, grabbed the pipe, and shuffled to where Cousin Jeff was pacing small circles on top of that piling.

"You jumped," he accused in a tight voice.

"But you said—"

"Only an idiot would believe me," he said. "You can't expect someone to actually jump from here."

I could feel a ball of stubbornness begin to build within me.

"I jumped. Now it's your turn."

In the end, Cousin Jeff refused. I jumped again, just to show it could be done, but even after I returned for the second time—now too angry to notice the danger of holding on to the pipeline as I crossed beneath the bridge—Cousin Jeff would not jump.

There may or may not be a moral in my bridge jumping, but I did learn something powerful that day. Yes, it was crazy of me to jump, and yes, I would like to be able to blame it on Cousin Jeff.

But, of course, it was my decision, and of course, I'd done it because I thought I had to prove something. That reason itself was far more stupid than jumping off the bridge.

I've since discovered that the really strong, really secure people don't have the need to prove anything. They know within themselves what they can and cannot do, and that is enough. So they do what they do—in every field from motherhood, to policework, to doctoring—with quiet, self-assured confidence and, yes, gentleness and compassion, because all of that takes a great deal of strength.

In sports, too, I've discovered it is the quiet ones you need to fear.

In racquetball, the guys with the flashy equipment and great stories—they were the guys trying to make up for a lack of ability. The players with the old wrinkled gloves, wrinkled clothes, and the small smiles waited until the game to prove themselves. And when it was over, they had no need to brag. Their actions had spoken loud enough.

In hockey, the guys who always made a big deal of offering to fight—they were the ones who somehow managed to get behind a protective referee when it really counted. The others, the truly tough ones, never needed to show they were tough. They just didn't back down when someone pushed them too far.

Those without confidence? They spend a lot of time faking it, which usually involves acting as macho as possible, giving or accepting dares.

Bridge-jumping that day wasn't all bad, though. One result was that it gave me a lot of freedom. I keep that memory in the back of my mind whenever I feel the stupid urge to prove something to someone simply for the sake of proving it.

The other result was even better.

Cousin Jeff never risked our lives again.

THE BANKER DOWN THE STREET

2

Nobody, especially not Joel, should be able to make paper planes from my baseball cards and get away with it. Which was why I was stomping through the neighborhood, determined to fold Joel in a few different directions.

Joel is my six-year-old brother, who haunts me worse than any ghost. Even though I'm twelve, he terrifies me. Somehow he appears and disappears when I least expect or want it. Walls and locked doors don't stop that kid. When I do spot him—which is rare—he says nothing. He just stares at me with solemn eyes that take in exactly whatever I'm doing at that moment, which usually happens to be something I want nobody in the world to see. Then, as I'm bursting out of my skin with surprise at his sudden appearance, he's gone again.

Is he tough to find when you want him? That's like asking how easy it'd be to catch a hummingbird with your arms tied behind your back.

I knew I was finally getting close to Joel, because I had checked all the yards except for Mr. Frederick's. Joel might be like a ghost, but even he is smart enough to stay out of *that* yard. Mr. Frederick is an old retired banker, and he hates kids, dogs, ice cream, laughter, and anything else fun.

I closed my eyes to concentrate, and something tapped

me on the shoulder. I was too mad to jump with fright—the way I usually do when Joel sneaks up—so I whirled around and hissed, "Jerk!"

But it wasn't Joel. It was a bearded man with skin almost red-bronze from the sun. Grown-ups are hard to judge for age, but I guessed him at twenty-five.

"How can you say that?" He smiled to interrupt my coughing fit of embarrassment. "You don't even know me."

"I didn't mean to call *you* a jerk," I began.

He waved it away. "I gathered you were looking for someone else."

I nodded.

He continued to smile. "Can you point me to Harold Frederick's house?"

"Sure," I said. "But even if I was related, I wouldn't go there."

"Why?" Still the man's smile continued.

"He's mean. Mean as a box of angry snakes, my dad says. And my dad hates saying bad things about people."

"I'm not related," the man said. "I've got a letter for him. From India. . . ." His smile twisted, like he was trying to make me curious. It worked.

"India?"

"Yup. India. Want to help me deliver this?"

He looked big enough to protect me. I nodded.

Mr. Frederick had wire-frame glasses and a few strands of gray, wispy hair. He was sitting on his porch, guarding his lawn against dogs and kids.

He grunted as we approached.

"Mr. Frederick, I have a letter for you," the man said.

"So?"

"It's from your brother." That sent chills down my spine.

The story was that Mr. Frederick's brother had disappeared at least fifty years ago.

"My brother left years ago," Mr. Frederick snorted. "If he hasn't cared enough to say where he went by now, why should I care about him? And what's that kid doing with you?"

"He's showing me around. I'm on my way home from India. This town wasn't far out of my way. And I was curious about this letter."

"I'm not," Mr. Frederick said.

The bearded man smiled at Mr. Frederick. "This letter is a half-century old."

Mr. Frederick sat straight up.

"Yes," the man said. "I like to travel. I was in the Himalaya Mountains, near Mount Everest. I was in a village so remote that children touched my white skin to see if it was real. And an old man called me into his hut. It took a while to understand, but finally I knew what he was trying to tell me. It was about this letter."

Joel and paper plane baseball cards were definitely not a priority anymore.

"The old man had been a guide when he was young, carrying equipment for people going into the mountains. He explained that one man, a white man, had died after falling and breaking his leg. The guides divided his equipment among themselves. The old man had taken a leather pouch as part of his share, and in it he found this letter.

"He was too scared to throw away a white man's words and felt too guilty for stealing that man's equipment to send it. So he kept the letter. But it was on his conscience for so long that he cried with relief when I accepted it from him."

The man paused.

"This letter was addressed to you, Harold Frederick."

"So give it to me and scram," Mr. Frederick said.

"But he came all this way," I said.

"You scram, too."

The man gave the letter to Mr. Frederick, then smiled at me and put his hand on my shoulder. "No problem, kid. Let's go."

When we reached the sidewalk again the man said to me, "Don't worry about people like him. He's missing so much in life, it's punishment enough."

I nodded, not quite understanding.

"And if you're looking for a kid half your size, he's hiding in a garbage can two houses back."

That was the last I saw of the bearded stranger.

I banged on the garbage can to give Joel a good scare, then bought him an ice-cream cone. I had too much to think about to be mad anymore.

The funny thing was, later that afternoon when we accidentally hit a baseball into Mr. Frederick's yard, he didn't come out and yell at us. He just stood on the porch with a strange look on his face and watched us run away.

The next day everyone in town thought Mr. Frederick had gone crazy.

First he threw out all his umbrellas. Right into the middle of the street. Then he bought a motorcycle and roared up and down the streets of Jamesville for a few hours. After that he visited the music store and the flower store, two places, my mom said later, that he had never visited before in his life.

Joel and I would also have thought he was crazy, except for one thing. We were down by the creek cooling our feet in the water when Mr. Frederick walked past us with a saxophone and a bundle of flowers.

What he did when he reached the creek at first made me think he *had* gone crazy. There was a small dam, built from bricks and stones a long, long time ago. It was crumbling and falling apart. It didn't really stop water anymore, but it was a good way to cross the creek if you didn't mind falling in about half the time because of the loose stones.

First Mr. Frederick stared at the dam for a long time. Then he crossed it! He was so old he almost needed a cane, but instead he strapped the saxophone over his shoulder, held the flowers in one hand, and slowly tottered across. He nearly fell about six times, but finally he made it.

Mr. Frederick stayed on the path that led to the town cemetery, and Joel and I were too curious not to follow. Joel and I waited until he was out of sight, then followed him. I fell in the water. Joel didn't.

Mr. Frederick stopped at a grave near the edge of the cemetery, and what we heard next in the quiet air made it easy for Joel and me to become friends with Mr. Frederick later.

He carefully set the saxophone on the ground beside the grave and laid the flowers across the headstone.

"Mother, these flowers are from Jim," he said as he looked downward. "That's right. Jim. Your second son. My only brother. The one who always had a grin plastered on his face and was always moving, dancing like the wind. The one who laughed at my banking career. The one who never came back."

Mr. Frederick reached inside his coat pocket and pulled out the letter from India.

"He did write, Mother. Only it took a while getting here. And it seems he was smarter about living than I." Mr. Frederick paused. "A lot smarter—even though he died so soon. Let me read it to you, Mother."

Mr. Frederick began:

"'Harry, don't let God fool you with that tiny church building down the street. God is bigger than that. He is something to fill you with wonder, not something to make you wish the sermon was over. I knew it halfway up this mountain. Sky, snow, and the edge of forever. God fills all of it. Good thing, too. I need Him.

'Harry, I landed in boulders from twenty feet up and broke my leg in so many places there was nothing they could do. The road out is two weeks of walking away, and already my leg is black. Most of the time I'm too far gone to write.

'You're right, Harry. Trying to climb a mountain north of India is not sensible. Dying is not sensible. But I'm not sure how much "sensible" matters.

'Remember that day when we were boys? The day you decided not to cross the dam on the creek? I did, and I fell in. You watched and turned around. That's when we knew we were different. You became the banker. Safe and comfortable. And I couldn't get enough of God's world.

'Of course, you'll be the one to read Mom this letter. I'm sorry it became your job. Tell her it was worth it. I think that's what she wants to know.

'Tell her I wasn't stupid about taking chances. Tell her I know life is a gift from God and you shouldn't be stupid with it. This was just something that happened as I was taking that gift of life and using it as well as God would let me. I have the memories and scents of a thousand places. And He is in all of those places, Harry, not just in a small church building.

'You probably don't want advice from a younger brother. But listen anyway. Thirty more years of banking and as much time as you can cling to it in retirement is not enough. Take God's world and glory in it, even if you never leave banking or Jamesville. Time is forever, and what do those extra years count for if you do nothing with them? Don't become an old man with no memories.

'Forget your umbrella once in a while. Rain is okay.'"

That was all Mr. Frederick said into the quietness. He picked up his saxophone, and when he turned around he had a sad smile on his face. Joel and I stayed where we were for a long time after that, just thinking.

That night, Mr. Frederick began to play his saxophone on the front porch. People stopped to stare in amazement at the spectacle of old Harold Fredericks blowing notes. He acknowledged them by scowling in his usual way, and then by grinning, which wasn't usual.

It was just another thing to make people think he'd gone crazy. Joel and I knew better.

THE GREATEST GIFT:
Thoughts on *The Banker Down the Street*

S O THERE YOU ARE, walking down the street, and a limousine pulls up beside you. The chauffeur opens the rear door, an old man in an expensive suit gets out, hands you ten $100 bills, smiles, then gets back into the limo and rides out of your life.

One thousand dollars, just given to you. Then, almost before the limo's exhaust has cleared, you rip all those hundred-dollar bills into tiny pieces and let the wind blow them from your fingertips.

Crazy?

Probably. It's hardly likely that anyone would give you that kind of money, and, if it actually did happen, it's even less likely you'd throw it away.

Unfortunately, we too often do exactly that with the greatest gift given us: our lives.

I can imagine God with a clipboard, ticking off the list as He made us. "Hmm. Eyes to see. Ears to hear. Nose to smell. Fingertips and skin to feel. And let's not forget taste, either." He might continue down the clipboard. "Arms, legs, hands. Yup. Everything a person might need to get through life."

And finally He might reach the bottom of the clipboard. "Here's the important stuff. A brain to think and contemplate. And a soul to enjoy the give-and-take of love."

Most of us get all of that when we are born. For those who don't, the physical handicaps are challenges to be overcome, and there are many stories about the glorious ways that people overcome their difficulties. These people—the ones born blind, perhaps, or permanently hurt in accidents—are inspiring. They take what has been given them—far less than what has been given others—and use it to the best of their abilities. They *live* life.

How much more, then, should we live life, those of us who get the "full clipboard"? We can see, hear, taste, think, and love. How, then, can we throw away the gift of life—just as surely as ripping up hundred-dollar bills—by simply existing instead of joyfully exploring the world in which we live?

All of this was on my mind as I wrote *The Banker Down the Street. Wouldn't it be terrible,* I thought, *to become very old without having lived life?* Because then, when you look back on your life, you will see how you wasted all the gifts when you were young enough and strong enough to do something with them. Because then, when you look back, you will have too few memories of places and people, triumphs and defeats.

When I was eighteen, I had this foolish notion that a summer in France would be great fun. At that time Red Deer had a population of less than twenty-five thousand. It was so small it had only two movie theaters. France—in my mind day after day as I stocked shelves at a local grocery store—seemed an exciting place to be.

I knew some French, and I had romantic visions of me as the great wanderer, the mysterious stranger from a faraway land, so cool as I moved from town to town.

Wrong.

After I saved enough money from my job at the grocery store—dreaming of glory each day as I worked—I paid for the airfare and finally left home.

In France, much of the time I was miserable, scared, and homesick. Not much of a romantic vision at all. I traveled throughout the countryside by bicycle; dogs chased me often. Once, after riding hard all day, when all I wanted was a cold glass of milk and I had spent the last of my French currency on that milk, I gulped down half a quart before realizing it was sour. Another time a cyclist bumped me and I spilled into gravel. My hips and elbows were scraped so badly I bled for two days, and I still have the scars. I ran out of money. And every night I wondered why I wasn't enjoying the summer in Red Deer with my friends, doing the things we always did for fun. It would have been better if I'd traveled with someone. But none of my friends were stupid enough to go with me. So, in terms of *The Banker Down the Street*, it rained hard, and I had no umbrella.

Still, six weeks later when I returned home to the small prairie town—and believe me, I was happy to do so—I discovered something strange: If someone would have offered me the chance to go back in time and not go to France, where I was scared, miserable, and homesick, I would have refused. I would have done it all over again.

Why? I had memories of places and people that no photographs could ever capture. I had felt triumphs and despairs I would never have understood without leaving the security of my hometown. And I felt stronger for getting through those six weeks. It was a test that helped me prove something to myself.

In *The Banker Down the Street*, I was trying to explain that to Mr. Frederick. He, it seemed, was the type of person to frown upon anything unusual, the type of person who wanted life to be an orderly set of rules and regulations.

Life is not that way. Life is messy. Life is difficult. Life is not secure, no matter how much you try to make it secure. People lose jobs, people die in traffic accidents, people get their hearts broken, people make mistakes. Life is a wonderful voyage across uncharted waters. Rain lashes down one minute; other times sunshine breaks bright and warm through dark clouds.

What gives us strength is the knowledge that God is there during that storm. No matter what happens, He will receive us at the end. So, during the voyage, should we be huddled in the bottom of the boat, wrapped in five life preservers? Or should we be standing on the helm, shaking our fists at the rain and wind, or grinning in delight at the new and unexpected sights while the sun shines?

I don't want to mislead anyone (and perhaps *The Banker Down the Street* suggests it too easily) into believing that *travel* is the only way to explore life. Definitely not.

Anything you do—as long as you do it as well and as enthusiastically as possible—lets you explore life's ups and downs.

Travel is merely one way to explore. Getting married and raising a family is another way. Or taking a chance late in life on a new career. Or learning a new language. Or deciding to learn how to parachute. Or trying to become the next world champion tiddledywinks player. Anything but plodding through forty-hour workweeks and watching television every night.

Anything but throwing away the gift of life.

CELESTIAL C. MOONDUST

3

"Mike, I see you've lost your mind."

There was not much else to say. Not with him stripped down to gym shorts, soaked with water, and standing on a clay-splattered sheet of plastic in the corner of his laundry room.

Even on a normal day, half of Jamesville would agree with my assessment of Mike's mental state. They wouldn't blame it, though, on the wads of clay wrapped around his left arm. They'd probably say something had happened when he was a baby.

I passed those thoughts on to Mike.

"I was not dropped on my head at six months of age," he grunted as he continued to pack the clay around his left arm with an awkward one-handed movement of his right. "And call me crazy now, but I'll have the last laugh when I finally prove Celestial C. Moondust wrong."

Celestial C. Moondust. The new girl in our town of Jamesville.

Her real name, I happened to know, was Frieda Watson, but she insisted on calling herself Celestial C. Moondust. It was her spiritual name, she always said mysteriously.

Celestial was the spookiest twelve-year-old I knew. Black hair, black blouse, black dress, black socks, and black shoes. Every day she looked like that. Dark and forbidding. She also liked whispering chants to herself during the middle of class. She read vampire books and books on ancient Egyptian history. She had two sinister cats—black, of course—that followed her everywhere when she wasn't at school.

She was, in fact, so spooky that she nearly terrified me more than Joel, my six-year-old brother, who is like a ghost himself for the way he can sneak up on people.

To add to her spookiness, she had a crystal ball. And she had *The Hand.*

Which almost explained Mike's craziness.

Because *The Hand* was definitely the problem that went with Celestial C. Moondust.

"There is a dawning of the New Age," she always said whenever anyone at school teased her about her spookiness. "Remember *The Hand*, and know that spirits are upon us."

That usually silenced anyone. Because there was no way we could forget *The Hand*, not after she had brought it to school just to prove that spirits truly existed.

"Look at this," she had said that morning to Mike and me and a small group in the hallway before class. "Consider it proof that I'm right. Nothing but a spirit could have made this hand."

At first glance it didn't look like a big deal. It was a sculptured hand and forearm, exactly as if it had been cut off at the elbow. The hand was gracefully curved forward at the wrist. Even at second glance it hadn't been impressive.

Until she explained.

"This clay hand is hollow and wafer thin," she said, awe filling her voice.

"Staggering," Mike said with a low, sarcastic whistle. "*Hollow.* That proves a lot."

Her eyes flashed. "Obviously you're an imbecile. No sculptor in the world can fashion hollow fingers on the inside of clay by working from the outside."

She had a point.

Still, Mike snorted. "Who's the imbecile? Just wrap the clay around your hand. When you pull free, you've got a hollow hand and arm just like the one you pretend is so supernatural."

"Hah!" she said, pouncing. "That proves my point exactly. Your hand is wider than your arm. How do you intend to pull your hand free without breaking the narrower section of the clay arm?"

Mike opened his mouth to speak. Then snapped it shut. "She's right, you know," he whispered to me out of the side of his mouth.

"Of course I'm right." She smiled smugly. "It's all the proof you need to believe in spirits and visitors from another dimension. No human could have placed a hand inside clay and pulled it out later without breaking the mold."

Mike, for a change, had nothing to say.

Instead, he examined *The Hand* carefully.

Celestial finished, "*The Hand* was given to me as a going-away present from my spiritual advisor before I moved here. And she should know. She said it had materialized during a séance visitation when the spirit insisted on leaving something behind as proof."

With that and a flash of her dark eyes, Celestial calmly strode away, leaving Mike still speechless and very determined to prove her and her spirit world wrong.

So now it was a Saturday morning in the laundry room of his basement, and he was so determined to make his own version of *The Hand* that he didn't even realize he was shivering in the cold water that splashed around him as he kept the clay wet.

"Mike," I sighed. "Can't you let it rest? We already heard what our parents had to say. That proof is not the thing we should be worrying about."

His chin jutted. "We both know what we believe about God— that He's real, that He loves us." He held up his other arm, the one free of clay, and waved away my protests with a clay-smeared hand before I could even start. "And I know what we heard. That faith is not a matter of logic. Faith is believing without seeing, believing without proof."

I nodded impatiently. "Yes, Mike. But—"

"But nothing," he interrupted. "She runs around talking about spirits and other dimensions and tells everyone that *The Hand* shows she's right. That's how she's got proof spirits exist."

"So?" I said. "I don't believe her. You don't believe her."

"It still bugs me," Mike said with his typical stubbornness. "Maybe we don't have to prove God exists. But we *should* be able to prove that all her spirit stuff is wrong."

"By duplicating *The Hand.*"

Mike ignored the resignation in my voice. "I think I'm making progress," he said. "I've tried it four times already today. This time it should work. I greased my hand completely with graphite lubricant. The clay will dry, but the lubricant underneath won't."

"That's real exciting, Mike," I said. "Maybe this afternoon we can go outside and listen to your grass grow."

He frowned with concentration. "Shhhh. I think this mold around my arm is nearly ready. And my hand inside is slippery as snake oil. I'll just ease it out and—"

A huge crack split along the side of the clay molding as he tugged. "Nuts!" he said. "I'm going to try just one more time."

"Give up," I said.

"Are you saying you believe in her spirits?"

"No," I said. "But I don't think you need to prove anything to her."

Mike looked me straight in the eyes. "Ricky," he said, "you know how much I hate being serious. But this one has got me, pal. I looked at that stupid sculptured hand of hers closely. Real closely."

"And?" I stepped back, surprised at the trouble that showed across his face.

"There were no seams to show that it had been cut away from an arm and glued back together," he said quietly. "Nothing to show any possible way of making it. Please, please tell me how *The Hand* was made, pal. Because if you can't, I'm scared of what it might mean."

Normally you don't feel like thanking a six-year-old brother for getting you into enough trouble so that you have to load the dishwasher and scrub the supper pots and pans all by yourself. You feel less like thanking him when he sneaks up behind you to scare you half to death as you're doing those very same dishes.

But when it happened that Saturday after lunch, I felt like hugging the little rascal. Except by then, of course, he had disappeared again.

The trouble hadn't been major. I had hidden Joel's teddy bear because he had borrowed my comics. I got caught. He didn't. The story of my life. And Mom was probably looking for a good excuse to get me to do dishes anyway.

The jumping straight up in the air while doing dishes wasn't major, either. With a brother like Joel, you get used to it. When I landed, my comic books were on the floor beside me. Joel's way of apologizing.

But as I landed, scalding hot dishwater swished over the top of my rubber gloves and down into my hands. I had barely finished yelping with pain when a thought struck me, a thought that made me want to hug Joel with gratitude.

So after finishing the dishes I ran to a hardware store, then spent the rest of the Saturday afternoon busy in my basement.

"Frieda," I called down the hallway. There were ten minutes

until the nine-o'clock Monday morning math class began.

She ignored me.

"Frieda," I called louder.

"If you're speaking to me," she said with a toss of her long black hair, "the name is Celestial. Celestial C. Moondust."

I saw Mike behind her and waved him forward. He arrived just as I was saying, "I'm sorry, Frieda, but I don't believe in this spiritual name stuff."

"Remember *The Hand*." She smiled with a trace of arrogance.

Mike paled at the reference. Obviously he hadn't solved the problem.

"I remember it, all right," I said. By that time a few more people had gathered. I held a large bag carefully with both my hands. "In fact, I would like to introduce you to *The Hammer*."

She snorted. *"The Hammer."*

Her laugh ended quickly as I pulled the object from the bag in my hands.

It was a sculpted hammer. "It's made from hollow, wafer-thin clay," I said casually.

"It's ... it's ... it's supernatural," she breathed. "A symbol of great meaning left behind by a spirit."

Suddenly I didn't feel as triumphant as I had imagined. I was about to take away something she held very dear. An illusion.

"I'm sorry, Frieda," I said. "Actually, I made it myself."

She drew herself straight upright. "Impossible! Not hollow clay that thin." She held it and examined it. "No seams. No way of pulling the hammer loose from the setting clay without destroying the mold. It could only be a supernatural symbol. You are lucky, indeed, to receive a visit from the spirits."

I shook my head. "No supernatural symbol. Only wax and clay."

"No," she said. "No. No. No."

"I sculpted a hammer of wax. If you look closely, you can see I didn't do a good job. But the wax hammer was a good enough imitation for this. I then covered the wax hammer with clay. When the clay dried, I melted the wax out of the inside. Which, of course, left me with a hollow hammer." I looked into her dark eyes, and finished, "One made by human hands."

She shook her head wildly, then ran down the hallway.

I put my hand on Mike's arm as he moved to follow. "Talk to her later, Mike, when she's ready to listen."

He grinned at me. "How did you ever figure it out?"

"Joel," I said. "Because of him, I filled my rubber dish gloves with water. When I pulled my hands out of the gloves, the water still gave them shape. Then it hit me that you could fill the gloves completely, wrap them in clay, and pull the glove out later without breaking the mold. Which, of course, led me to think that a wax hand would work even better than a water-filled glove as a form to wrap. After all, wax melts long before clay."

"Good job, Ricky. You're a genius."

"I know," I started to say modestly. Then the school buzzer rang and Joel tapped my elbow from behind me at the same time, and from sheer surprise I dropped the hammer.

Bits of clay scattered from one side of the hallway to the other.

Mike laughed as he walked away. "Good job, Ricky. Like I said, you're a genius."

Right. The story of my life.

Is God Real?
Thoughts on *Celestial C. Moondust*

I GREW UP ON THE SOUTH part of town, which edged Bower's farm. The farm consisted of pastureland that held dozens of cows, thousands of gophers, and one or two of the nastiest bulls ever to snort and terrify a couple of kids who wandered too far away from the safety of the woods that bordered the fields.

Me and my bud Bruce—a phrase that drove Mom nuts because it was not grammatically correct—went "down the woods" of that farm every day after school in fall, winter, and spring, and spent most of our summer days, too, exploring the creek and the secret paths through the trees and brush.

It probably wasn't dangerous. But local legends held that Old Man Bower stalked those woods with a shotgun loaded with pepper and salt, determined to find and blast that salt and pepper into the hides of trespassing kids or, worse, tie them to trees and leave them there to be pecked to death by crows. (If you read the ACCIDENTAL DETECTIVES book *Phantom Outlaw at Wolf Creek,* you'll meet a hermit named Quigley. He's based on my memories and fears of Old Man Bower, who, by the way, never did catch us and, of course, was more fearful in legend than in real life.)

Despite the stories about Old Man Bower, we went. Me, Bruce, and frequently a couple of other kids. We went so often, we knew every inch of that area. We built a fort deep in a stand of spruce, a fort impossible for anyone else to find. And, about every two weeks in the summer (the time it took for us to forget how much the woods scared us at night), we would beg permission to go camping by ourselves.

We'd have a pup tent, sleeping bags, and enough hot dogs to make us sick. The big question we asked each other in the peacefulness of those nights—nights of stars so wonderful and far away, and coyotes returning our own howls cast at the moon—(before the *real* quiet time when the fire was dead and we were scared again)—was a question too many grown-ups try to ignore.

Is God real?

It was a logical question, away from all the distractions of daily life that tend to dull our senses to His presence. And to me, that question proves kids are smarter in a lot of ways than the grown-ups who worry so much about money, and bigger houses, and finding new ways to be entertained that they put that question aside.

Is God real?

It's the most important question in the world, the question you must answer before you can begin to ask any others.

If God truly is real, alive, and watching over us, it is an incredible comfort for all of us who believe in Him and His promises. If God truly is real, those choosing *not* to believe in Him will for all eternity be affected by their disbelief. If God truly is real, every question and decision you make must be asked and made with God's presence in mind.

However, if God is *not* real, as some claim, then life is a sad emptiness, and there is very little meaning in what we do. Life, then, is only a matter of living and dying, and who cares what happens between the two.

Is God real?

There are only two answers. Yes or no. One of the two. All of us have to decide at some time in our lives. Ignoring the question is just like choosing the answer "no." Deciding "yes" means trying to live life in a way that reflects that belief.

Is God real?

My answer to that question is yes, He is very real. But I can't *prove* it. No one can, and no one has been able to prove an answer—yes or no—since the first time that question was asked. Because of this, because "proof" of His existence has never been supplied, some people choose to believe that God is not real.

Of course, the obvious reply to someone who asks for proof of His existence is to ask for counterproof, proof that God does not exist. This has always led to long arguments and counter-arguments that ultimately go nowhere.

A major drawback to this standard circle of arguing God's existence or non-existence is in what people generally seek as proof: They want something they can see, touch, or hear.

In this short story, that's exactly what Celestial C. Moondust wanted as a basis for her beliefs. *The Hand* provided solid, earthly proof that her senses could not deny. (Mike fell into the same trap. Because he could see and touch *The Hand*, he held it to be "proof" and worried at the doubts it raised.)

During any struggle to question God's existence, it is really important to remember this: *As humans, our perception of reality is severely limited because of our reliance on our five senses.*

Take balloons, for example. If you've never done it before—and chances are you have—find a balloon, blow it up, and rub it vigorously against your hair. Then place the balloon against a wall.

What happens next? The balloon sticks to the wall, of course, and "mysteriously" stays suspended there.

Big deal, right? It's great for dazzling three-year-old brothers or sisters, but as party tricks go, this one's a dud. Not only has this trick been done hundreds of times, but most of your audience also knows the secret behind it: static electricity.

Did you know you can do this same sort of thing with amber? (Amber is fossilized tree sap hardened into a clear, yellowish material—like colored glass.) In fact, amber—not balloons—was the best party trick going from about 600 B.C. until A.D. 1700. Back in the time of the Greeks, people were aware of something very strange about amber. If they rubbed amber with a piece of fur, amber suddenly attracted small pieces of material—light cloth, feathers, stuff like that.

Why? Again, static electricity. The same thing that holds a balloon to the wall.

But to the Greeks, then to the Romans, then to the Anglo-Saxons, to the Europeans, and to every single culture since 600 B.C. this property of amber was incredible.

Despite the obvious answer to us now, for dozens of centuries people believed this strange magnetism was unique to amber, that amber and only amber could attract feathers. They had no idea that something called *electricity* existed.

It wasn't until Benjamin Franklin that our perception of this changed. Franklin, and another scientist, William Watson, concluded that all materials possess a kind of electrical fluid; rubbing merely transfers that "fluid," which we now know is electricity.

All right, already, you're probably saying to yourself. What do balloons, amber, and Benjamin Franklin have to do with Celestial C. Moondust and God?

Electricity itself has always existed. Yet for the bulk of mankind's history—*because electricity could not be perceived*—there was no *proof* of its existence. For the dozens of centuries until we finally found a way to measure electricity with our five senses, no one "believed" in it. But it was always there.

In other words, just because something is unseen, undiscovered, or unperceived, it is foolish to say it doesn't exist.

Is God real?

Because we cannot see, touch, or measure God, should we decide He does not exist beyond the limitation of our senses?

In fact, once you decide that "proof" of His existence is a foolish chase, then you can begin to be open to the things in life that point to Him with certainty—awe at the wide open night sky and its billions of stars, or awe at the intricacy of a spider web; the joy of unselfish love; the inner peace that comes from belief.

C. S. Lewis, who wrote the NARNIA CHRONICLES, calls this process "faith seeking understanding." Once you have faith, then your mind and imagination invites exploration of that faith, exploration of all that surely points to God. Mr. Lewis once wrote this: "I believe in Christianity as I believe the sun has risen, not only because I see it, but because by it I see everything else."

It seems to me that it ironically takes more faith to believe that there is *no* God. After all, you have to be a very determined nonbeliever in the face of the wonders of this world to believe it all started by accident or happenstance.

Even something that happens as often as the birth of a child is a miracle. Doctors and scientists can detail—stage by stage—the prebirth development of a baby, yet they are unable to explain exactly how or why the first few cells of the embryo have that first spark of life to start the process.

Is God real?

No matter how much those around you might push you to believe—or to disbelieve—it is a decision only you can make for yourself.

Approach the question with an open heart and open mind.

Don't bind yourself with limited definitions of proof.

The God you will begin to understand and know is not a puny God who conveniently fits into whatever box we want to place Him in. But He is as big as forever, mightier than the worst storms and earthquakes you can imagine, and more wonderful than the starry diamonds He has placed in a clear night sky.

MAGIC PENNIES 4

I had to be careful in spots along my paper route. If Old Man Jacobsen caught me saving steps by cutting across his lawn, he yelled—loud. And Mr. Thompson, who owned the only corner store in Jamesville, didn't like it when I crawled through the hole in his hedge.

At least the Bradleys and Trentons were never home until supper, so I could balance my shortcut across the top of their tall fence without worry. The dogs in both their yards always jumped and scratched and barked themselves silly against the fence, but it didn't bother me. I just knew I'd aim myself for the Trentons' yard if I ever fell, because on the Bradley side lived the German shepherd who hated me for squirting his mouth with a water pistol whenever he barked at me.

Yup. I had all the tricks and shortcuts figured out along my paper route, and only one person made me nervous.

My kid brother, Joel, of course.

I will admit, though probably not to Mom or Dad, that there are times—only occasionally—on my paper route when I need to leave areas quickly.

This time it was a case of not watching my step. Mrs. Henry has a stubborn fat cat that never moves from her sidewalk. I accidentally stepped on its tail for the fourteenth day in a row. Over the yowl I heard a creaking of Mrs. Henry's screen door. It seemed best to walk fast and not look back. And, I rehearsed my excuse, how could anyone hear Mrs. Henry yelling over the noise the cat made?

I got around a corner and closed my eyes for a split second to relax.

Someone tapped my elbow. I nearly jumped into a tree, paper bag and all. It was Joel. He didn't say anything, just stared. He likes cats.

That did it. I had to find a way to stop him from following me. Just as my heart slowed down, an idea hit me. I straightened out my papers and turned to talk to Joel.

He was gone.

It didn't matter. I whistled the rest of my route and didn't take any more shortcuts. I'd catch him at home.

After supper, as usual, Joel disappeared. Just disappeared. So I went to Joel's hiding spot for his teddy bear.

The teddy bear is his only weakness. If he was asleep, you could have a circus band in the room, or a good-smelling hot dog two inches in front of his nose, and he wouldn't wake up. But touch the teddy bear, and his eyes pop open. It's easy to find the bear. Joel thinks if he covers the teddy bear's eyes, nobody can see it.

I wriggled one paw. Somehow, thirty seconds later, Joel stood in front of me, staring mournfully.

"Ever wonder why I do papers?" I asked.

He shook his head.

"Let me tell you anyway," I said.

He yawned and started to walk away. I put a stranglehold on his teddy bear. He decided to listen.

I told Joel that people who want newspapers have magic pennies. These pennies grow in their mailboxes, one penny a day. Paperboys simply trade a paper for each penny. And I showed Joel a shiny copper penny.

His eyes opened wide in delight to see the penny, and he stuck out a tiny hand. I put the penny in his palm.

"Tomorrow," I said, "you can do half my houses and keep the pennies for yourself."

Joel nodded excitedly. I sneezed from the dirt on his teddy bear, and when I opened my eyes, Joel was gone.

Later that night I told Mom that Joel would be helping me with papers. Grown-ups can sometimes be funny about good ideas, so I told her when she was on the phone. She might not have listened to me too well—another rehearsed excuse—but at least I had told her.

The idea worked great.

I have forty houses on my route and get paid a dime a paper each day. Running ahead with twenty pennies to put in the mailboxes of half the route took only a few minutes.

It took Joel a lot longer to deliver the papers. He knew the route better than I did from always following me, but the papers were heavier for him and he had to walk slower.

That kept him out of my hair. My own twenty papers took hardly any time, especially without the extra weight of Joel's papers. I had my usual shortcuts, too, and I didn't have to worry about Joel around the next corner waiting to pop me out of my shoes with surprise.

I also made nine cents on each paper he delivered. It felt good to be a smart businessman. My conscience kept trying to remind me of something, but the idea was foolproof, and I was paying him more money than he had ever made before, so I did my best to ignore it.

This idea worked so smoothly, I considered upping Joel's load to thirty papers. I'm glad I waited, though, or I would have felt even worse than I did on my birthday.

The way it worked at our house was that you had to wait until supper to open presents so that Dad could be there after work. You even had to wait until after dessert, so that everyone would give the present-opening their full attention. It really just meant we never really tasted our dessert on the day of our birthday.

Mom and Dad gave me great presents, but something was missing. That something was Joel. Usually he would creep close and get in the way because he always believed there would be something for him.

"Where's Joel?" Dad asked.

Mom beamed with pride. "Joel's becoming a big boy. He realizes that presents are just as much fun to give as get."

The little kid floored me. He appeared from behind my chair and shyly handed me a box.

"Yes, Ricky," Mom said. "Joel made me take him to the store yesterday and help him buy something for you. I don't know where it came from, but he had a jarful of shiny pennies, and he wouldn't let us leave until he spent all of them."

I unwrapped a brand-new baseball and a pack of gum. Joel smiled and patted my knee before vanishing under the tablecloth.

My throat hurt so bad I could hardly speak, so I didn't. I managed not to cry until I was by myself.

The next day I told Joel to look for dimes, and sure enough he began to find them in the mailboxes. I would walk with him for all of his twenty houses each day and carry the papers for him.

When we finished his papers I would do my own. Of course,

freed from his work, he began following me again in his terrifying way.

Maybe he found it strange that I could be so nice day after day. But I didn't care. Every time I saw that baseball, I realized how wrong I had been and how much it meant to have him for a brother.

Then one day someone tapped my shoulder as I began my treacherous crawl through the hole in Mr. Thompson's hedge. My crawl became a leap, and even as I was jumping straight up into the middle of the hedge, I knew it could only be Joel.

By the time he helped me pick up every page of every newspaper, he knew I was his normal grumpy big brother again.

PANGS OF THE HEART:
Thoughts on *Magic Pennies*

MONEY IS EXTREMELY IMPORTANT in this world.
Money, however, is not "the root of evil," as you might often hear, for that is a misquote from the tenth verse of 1 Timothy, chapter 6, in the New Testament of the Bible. Money itself is necessary, and often capable of great good.

The complete quote is: "For *the love of money* is the root of all evils; it is through this craving that some have wandered away from the faith and pierced their hearts with many pangs" (RSV).

This is a passage that must fill any writer with admiration. The words are poetic and stirring, and the passage also speaks two great truths in few words.

Indeed, the love of money leads some people to eighty- or ninety-hour workweeks, constant and exhausting business trips, ulcers and heart problems from stress as they sacrifice families and health for huge corporate salaries. The love of money leads others to lie, steal, or cheat, to betray friendships and integrity; it even leads to murder in the darker shadows of the criminal world. The love of money leads yet others—some of the fortunate and already wealthy—to hoard their money when it is capable of doing great good around them.

Yes, it is difficult to deny that most of the minor and major evils in our world can be traced back to the love of money.

Ricky Kidd discovers the other truth of that passage, too, when Joel gives him a new baseball in *Magic Pennies*. When easy money blinds you, the result of the love of money too often is a heart pierced with many pangs.

Why is it so easy to love money? Because from the first time someone puts a quarter in our tiny hands and lets us choose our own candy at a store counter, we see the power of money and see that there is a limited amount of money to spend.

As a result, in a world where nearly everything has a price tag— from chewing gum and toys to salaries to charities to welfare programs—we are conditioned very early to ask the big money question: How much money will it cost me?

Yet, when the love of money is so dangerous and can lead to so much pain, and as we face the price tags all around us, I think we forget too often to ask a bigger and more important question:

How much will my money cost me?

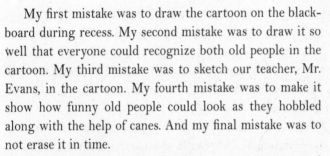

My first mistake was to draw the cartoon on the black-board during recess. My second mistake was to draw it so well that everyone could recognize both old people in the cartoon. My third mistake was to sketch our teacher, Mr. Evans, in the cartoon. My fourth mistake was to make it show how funny old people could look as they hobbled along with the help of canes. And my final mistake was to not erase it in time.

So when Mr. Evans walked into the classroom and looked at the sketch of him and his bald head and bloodshot eyes and big nose with a wart added for special effect, there was nearly a half minute of terrible silence. Except, of course, for the thundering of my heart.

Why did I do this?

After the agony of all that waiting, he did not ask who was responsible. Instead, Mr. Evans directed a question to our whole class. "Who's looking forward to vacation?"

We all stuck up our hands.

I never even had a chance to confess. Mr. Evans saw the white chalk all over my fingers and knew right away I had sketched that cartoon.

Of course, I should have known something would go wrong when even Joel snickered at my practice cartoons at home. His favorites, like mine, were the ones of Mr. Evans and his friend, Old Man Jacobsen.

Old Man Jacobsen lives just down the street in our town of Jamesville. He has the kind of yard that a lot of old people seem to have. It is always neat, with the grass cut short. He has two big trees in the front, and another tree with crab apples. He yells if he sees you trying to climb his trees or if you accidentally hit the tree with a stick just to see if the apples are loose. Fortunately, he can't see much because his glasses are so thick, and he can't run real fast, so my friends and I never worry about him getting us into too much trouble.

His friend Mr. Evans lives close to our school. Good thing, because Mr. Evans has been teaching there forever, and if he and his cane had to walk farther than a block to get to school, he might never make it. Naturally, his yard is neat, too, which makes me mad because whenever my dad sees it, he remembers to make me mow our own grass again.

Mr. Evans has to use a hearing aid when he teaches. It's hard to tell who is older, him or Old Man Jacobsen, even when you see them together.

They walk up and down the street a lot around suppertime on those warm days when the air is so quiet it almost feels soft.

Both of them together could never sneak up on anybody. Mr. Evans thinks because he can barely hear, nobody else can, so he talks loud. He's always yelling for Old Man Jacobsen to watch out through those thick glasses for another bump in the sidewalk. And Old Man Jacobsen always yells out "Thank you" back into Mr. Evans' hearing aid.

Watching the two of them bumble down the street was so much like watching a cartoon that all I ever had to do was close my eyes to see them. And that led, of course, to the sketches.

I would draw the big trees on the street and the sidewalks. Then I would put two men there. They would be hunched over a bit and using canes. After I practiced a lot you knew it was them, especially when I got good enough to make it look like they were yelling at each other. The fun part was adding the warts and single hairs that wavered like antennas from their bald heads.

Naturally, I had to share these sketches. Which led to the artwork during recess, artwork sprawled across one entire chalkboard.

Why hadn't I erased the sketch in time? Mostly because everyone had been laughing so hard, we didn't hear the usual squeaking of Mr. Evans' shoes as he approached, then stepped into the classroom to shock all of us into silence.

And that led, of course, to Mr. Evans seeing the chalk on my fingers and knowing exactly who had been making fun of them.

He pointed at me and asked me to stand.

"Ricky Kidd," he said. "Perhaps you should erase your handiwork."

I gulped and then erased. Even wiping the board sounded loud in that classroom.

Then he looked at me sternly. "Ricky, I will be asking you to do me a favor tomorrow."

I nodded.

He continued. "But not without your parents' permission."

Even before they heard from Mr. Evans, Mom and Dad found Joel under the couch coloring on a few of the drawings I had left at home. He was humming as he colored, so for a change he wasn't hard to find.

My dad asked, "Is this Mr. Evans and Old Man—I mean, Mr. Jacobsen?"

"Yes," I said.

He smiled just a bit until he saw Mom watching. Then he grunted a little. "Make sure Joel doesn't give them a copy."

"Too late," I mumbled to myself. "Far too late for that."

My dread made supper hard to chew. The phone rang as I picked at dessert, and when Dad had to hold the phone back from his ear and yell back, I knew Mr. Evans was on the other end.

Dad looked at me as he talked. "Yes, Mr. Evans. That shouldn't be a problem. I'll be happy to arrange that tomorrow."

Dad hung up the phone.

"Does 'sorry' help?" I asked.

He shook his head. But instead of a lecture, he ignored me and spoke to Mom. "I'll need a hand getting a few things ready for Ricky's morning at school."

She started to ask why.

"I'll explain later," he said with a little smirk, "after our famous artist son Leonardo da Vinci here is asleep."

And that's all I knew about the phone call.

As I fell asleep that night, I heard the whirring of the sewing machine.

The next morning Dad explained the rules to me at breakfast. "Ricky, Mr. Evans wants only three things from you today. One, he wants you to promise to wear three items until lunchtime and, two, not tell anybody about them."

I looked at what Dad had arranged beside my bowl of cornflakes.

Eyeglasses, earplugs, and some lumpy armbands?

"What is all—"

"Then he wants you to do a half hour of reading after school."

Despite my puzzlement, I grinned my best grin. For a while I thought I had been in serious trouble. Everybody knew how much I liked reading. And of the three things I had to wear to school, people would only notice the glasses. This punishment looked easy.

It didn't take me long to find out how wrong I was.

I got teased a bit about the glasses, but that didn't matter much compared to the problem they gave me in seeing. Everything was blurry.

I kept my promise about wearing them. They made me walk real slow, because it was so blurry I never knew where I was going. I'm also not sure of anything that happened that morning, because I could barely read the blackboard.

Not only that, but I could hardly hear Mr. Evans or anybody else. Mom and Dad had carefully installed cotton and ear plugs before I left for school, and because of the hair over my ears, nobody noticed. Except me. It was tough to hear anything except loud words.

My friend Mike got pretty mad because he thought I was ignoring him. I would hear some noise behind my desk like a bunch of whispering, and then he would poke me. It was a mad poke, too. Finally he quit.

The worst part was going out at recess time and trying to play baseball. Underneath my clothes I wore some weights that Mom had sewn into bands of cloth to go around my waist and also around my ankles.

Not only was I deaf and blind, but I was slow. Then it hit me. I was nearly deaf and blind.

Just like some old people.

Realizing what Old Man Jacobsen and Mr. Evans had to go through was such a surprise, I didn't even mind being the slowest guy on the field.

My friends had a laugh at how clumsy I was that day. But I kept my promise and didn't tell them why it was so hard to play regular baseball.

The part that got to me most that day was to hear the mixture of happiness and sadness in Mr. Evans' voice after school as he gave me instructions on the other part of what I had to do for him.

He said, "I want you to stop by the library and ask Mrs.

Reynolds for these high school yearbooks."

I nodded and took the piece of paper with the years of the requested books written on it. The yearbooks were more than fifty years old.

My ears were now unplugged, the weights gone from my arms, but with the memories of my struggles, Mr. Evans didn't seem so strange and far away and old to me anymore.

He continued with the same happiness and sadness of memories in his voice. "Ricky, find those yearbooks and look up a fellow named Jim. His last name is Jacobsen. I want you to know he is a good friend of mine, and I'm very proud of him."

It took a while for Mrs. Reynolds to find those books. She wiped dust off the covers and handed them to me with a quizzical look.

I didn't explain why I needed them.

When I found the right pages, I recognized Old Man Jacobsen in the photos immediately, even though he was just a kid and looked strange in those old-fashioned gym clothes.

There he was with a grin that was shy because of the pretty cheerleader beside him. But it was also a big grin because of the basketball trophy he was holding together with another boy named Jeff Evans. They were both captains of the high school basketball team.

In the photos—and I found lots of others showing football, baseball, band, and more—their hair was thick and dark, and handsome eyes twinkled in unwrinkled faces. The two young men looked like they thought they could conquer the world.

And then I thought of the cartoon in my head, how the friends, so many years later, still went for their walks together. You can bet after that day I always enjoyed hearing those two shout at each other as they slowly moved down the sidewalks of Jamesville.

WHO WILL YOU BE?
Thoughts on *Old Friends*

BABIES AND OLD PEOPLE are different species of human beings than the rest of us.

That's my theory.

Species, as defied by my Oxford dictionary, is "a class of things having some common characteristics." Wolves and foxes are *different* but *related* species, as are elephants and rhinos.

And, as you may know, scientists have defined us humans as the *homo sapiens* species, but they have not been wise enough to subdivide us further.

Thus, I gladly propose a more accurate form of classification: 1. Homo sapiens *fullias-diaperous*; 2. Homo sapiens *normalus*; and 3. Homo sapiens *raisin-wrinkulus*.

Why?

While all three species have "common characteristics"—two arms, two legs, same general shape, and the rest—that's where the similarities end.

Try talking to a homo sapiens *fullias-diaperous*. If you're lucky you'll get an enthusiastic "goo-goo" or a rattle shake in response. If you're unlucky, you'll have to dodge spit-up. It doesn't make for meaningful dialogue.

In short, there is such a gulf between you and a baby, for all practical purposes, you are a different species.

The same goes for the older species, homo sapiens *raisin-wrinkulus.*

Sure, old people can at least say words we might be able to understand. But how often do the words they choose make sense?

They want to talk about lessons learned (what do they know, anyway?), memories past (not again, the story about walking five miles to school in waist-deep snow), and, over and over, you will hear them say they simply do not understand the younger generation. (Can we help it they were born before television was invented?)

Furthermore, old people have no sense of what is fashionable; they move slower than us, and they actually drink prune juice without someone forcing them to do so.

Yup, a totally different species.

That, at least, was Ricky Kidd's initial perception of Mr. Evans and Old Man Jacobsen.

I hardly blame him. Let's face it, unless we're lucky enough to have a special grandparent or other older friend in our lives, how often do we share enough time with someone of that generation to understand what it is like to be truly old?

When I wrote *Old Friends*, I was nearly thirty. (If you think that's approaching ancient, try imagining what it would be like to be seventy.) At age thirty, I was just beginning to realize that I would not be young forever. For example, when I played racquetball in tournaments, the twenty-year-old players drove me nuts—they could run all day without getting tired or raising a sweat. Unlike before, when *I* was the one playing old coots who were thirty, suddenly I had become the victim gasping between rallies.

Not only that, at thirty I actually began to look forward to Sunday afternoons so that I could have a nap—just like the way I remembered my dad did.

As it slowly dawned on me that I, too, would become an old person—hopefully, if I lived that long—I began to study with great interest the species homo sapiens *raisin-wrinkulus*.

And I began to wonder about my upcoming transition into the next species. After all, babies eventually become us, and we eventually become old people.

Babies, of course, have no choice about the direction of their development. Properly loved, properly fed, and properly raised, they become great children, teenagers, and adults. But poorly loved, poorly raised, and ignored too long, babies have a real tough time as they grow older.

Babies are completely helpless and can only accept the treatment given them. On the other hand, who *we* become as we grow older is entirely up to us. Not only can we take responsibility for the physical elements that affect us—food, exercise, and hygiene—but we can make choices about our education, actions, and personality.

In other words, who we will be as individuals in the future depends completely upon how we live today.

That single, unarguable fact has led me to two perspectives—each as far apart from the other as possible.

With one perspective, I focus on *today* and look *forward*. Where will my immediate choices take me?

Sometimes the shortcuts aren't in my best interests. A year ago, when my dentist told me I should have my wisdom teeth removed, I was reluctant. The operation would cost a thousand dollars; I would be in terrible pain for a week, and besides, my wisdom teeth weren't bothering me. When he told me that trouble would surely arrive within ten years, and that an operation then had a good chance of leaving my face paralyzed, I decided I should be looking down the road. The wisdom teeth were removed—I was right, it did hurt like crazy—but now I'm glad it's over with.

You may not be worried about your wisdom teeth right now, but you might be asking yourself whether you want to spend four or five years in college or go to work from high school. Here's a big decision that will greatly change your life in the long run. Yet either direction may be right for you.

I think, however, it is the sum total of all your little choices that are the most important. Yes, *what you do for a living* is certainly a big factor in your life, but *who you are* is infinitely more important. And who you are is the combination of years of small moral choices.

Tell a little lie to escape a little trouble, or take responsibility for your actions? After ten years of tiny lies, without knowing it, you become a person no one trusts.

Avoid a little extra work, or do the job properly? After ten years of small decisions to be lazy, suddenly you're the kind of person who never gets anything done.

Unfortunately, I happen to prefer the easy way and the short-cuts. It takes real effort to remind myself that making the tougher decision today is simply an investment in my future. I haven't always avoided those tempting shortcuts, but every time I have, I've not regretted the extra effort.

So that's one way to make decisions: look forward from today.

More fun for me is the second perspective I've taken since beginning to study the species of old people. Instead of focusing on today and looking forward, I focus on a faraway *tomorrow* and look *backward*. In other words, I'll pretend I'm already old. Not only does it make life more fun, but it takes a lot of my worries away.

I often ask myself, as a seventy-year-old sitting in a rocking chair, what would I think about my decision today as a forty-four-year-old? In other words, how will I feel about my choice over a quarter century later? Will the old person I become approve or disapprove of my decision when he looks back?

For me, if I think the seventy-year-old me in the rocking chair would smile in memory, I'll usually do it.

If I think the seventy-year-old me in the rocking chair wouldn't even be able to remember the decision, I'll realize the decision obviously isn't important enough to agonize over.

If I think the seventy-year-old me in the rocking chair would be sad that it was an inconsiderate or selfish choice, I'll do my best to change the choice.

A fun perspective? You bet. For example, with that attitude, I made a really "stupid" decision when I was in my late twenties. I had always dreamed about crossing Canada on a bicycle. To do so made little sense. I should have been working that summer because I needed the money to finish the university. The trip would be three months of solitude, away from my friends. And what would my reward be? To most people, probably just tired legs and debt.

But I figured when I was seventy, and probably far too old to depend on my legs to pedal me four thousand miles across mountains, prairie, and the rest of Canada, then in that old rocking chair I would be happy that I'd taken advantage of younger legs and tasted the freedom of the wind in my face with no idea where the day might take me.

So I went.

Years have passed, and the painful sacrifice of considerable money spent has long been forgotten. But the memories of what I saw will be with me always.

It works the other way, too. I'll try to let the "seventy-year-old me" keep me in check. For example, what if—when making the same decision on that bike trip—I'd have had to abandon a wife and small children to take the same three months to cross Canada? Then the seventy-year-old me in the rocking chair would have been sad at my selfishness, no matter how glorious the adventure. And, I hope and believe, my decision would have then been no, remain at home.

One last thing about growing old.

Someone once said that at fifty, everyone has the face he or she deserves.

Look around and see for yourself. Grumpy old people? They've frowned so many thousands of times that the skin on their faces has been trained to arrange itself in wrinkles that form a frown, and they look grumpy, even when they're not.

Nasty people have had nasty expressions so often that their faces at rest look nasty.

Selfish people look selfish.

The nice thing is that it works the other way, too. So start smiling.

Nothing like the flicking of a snake's tongue and the evil you imagine in the snake's thick black body to get your attention before school even starts for the day.

The good thing about the snake was that it was in a small aquarium with a screen on top. The bad thing was that Butch Dolby was carrying the aquarium. His big brother had caught the snake for him to use on a science project.

And, with about five minutes before classes started, Butch was chasing everyone with the aquarium, laughing at how everyone screamed and ran from him.

As long as I've known him, he's been called Butch. Sometimes people have names that don't match, like the way everybody calls Harvey Voortel "Shorty" because he's the biggest. But in Butch's case, the name fits.

Butch is nearly as big as Harvey Voortel. But unlike Harvey, Butch is mean and takes advantage of his size. He's even proud to be known as "Butch the Bully." The only person who scares him is Harvey.

When Harvey is not around, Butch will gladly punch you in the shoulder, right where it hurts the most. Or he will push your face into the wall until you say "uncle." Or he will grab your chocolate bar and dare you to say something while he eats it. If you ever tell the teacher, Butch gets you back later, except much worse.

I thought we were saved when Harvey walked around the corner of the school. Most of the time, he's the only thing to slow Butch down.

Harvey watched for a bit, then said, "Hey, Butch, knock it off." Harvey is always quiet, so when he talks most of us pay attention.

Butch stopped and looked at him. "Oh yeah, make me."

That was surprising. Normally Butch was scared because they were about the same size. Until he held a snake as a weapon.

Butch walked closer to Harvey. "Come on," Butch said. "Make me." All of the rest of us got quiet. If Harvey lost to Butch, we'd never be safe.

Harvey made the mistake of stepping back as Butch held the aquarium high into his face. I didn't blame him. The snake was pushing hard against the glass, head raised high, flicking that tongue in and out.

"I said knock it off." Harvey edged back again.

Butch said, "Try anything and I'll open this cage so fast, you'll think twenty snakes hit you."

When Harvey didn't say anything, Butch knew he'd won. And his plan would have worked perfectly, except for one thing.

In his eagerness to finally scare Harvey, he moved forward a little too quickly, and he tripped over a bump. The aquarium flew straight up into the air, then crashed down beside Butch. He rolled over to try to get up and almost landed right on top of the snake. Suddenly the snake shot right on top of him.

The snake slithered up his jacket, then stopped, face to face with Butch, who was now on his back, legs and arms stiff and straight with fear. All that came from Butch's throat was a gurgle.

We were all too scared to help.

The snake remained staring as it flicked that tongue in and out, inches away from Butch's eyes. I almost felt sorry for him.

"Help me, someone please help me." Butch's voice was barely a moan.

I felt a gentle pluck on my coat sleeve. Joel had arrived with his usual quiet curiosity. He paused as he surveyed the situation, came to whatever mysterious conclusions fill his head, then left my side, calmly walked to Butch, and grabbed the snake right behind its head.

The snake seemed bigger than Joel's arm, and when he carried it, part of its wriggling tail dragged on the ground.

That night Joel explained it to me by simply stating, "Bull snake." I had to go to the library the next day to find out bull snakes weren't poisonous. How Joel knew is beyond me, unless Old Man Jacobsen taught him on one of their nature walks.

At the time Joel was definitely the only one to know. Everybody gave him and the dragging snake a wide berth. Joel took the snake to the edge of the playground near a stand of trees, set it down, and watched it scoot into the deep grass.

Anybody else would have pretended like it was a big deal, but to anybody else it *would* have been a big deal. Joel, I'm sure, forgot about it by lunchtime and didn't remember until I had a chance to ask him about it that night.

No one else forgot, though, not during school hours.

"Hey, Butch. Hey, fraidy-cat Butch. Good thing a little kid rescued you. Nyah, nyah, nenyahnyah."

"Butch, watch out for that spider! Nyah, nyah, nenyahnyah."

"Hey, Butch, isn't it time for a nap? Your mommy wants you to grow big and strong someday. Nyah, nyah, nenyahnyah."

I think it was the "nyah, nyah, nenyahnyahs" that were the worst for Butch. All day it continued. Whenever anyone, even the smallest person in the class, thought of a good way to bug Butch, they did, and everyone within hearing distance would laugh and laugh and laugh.

I got my shots in, too. "Hey, Butch, if you want, I'll ask Joel to be your bodyguard. Nyah, nyah, nenyahnyah."

When he looked up at all of us laughing, I caught a sad look in his eye, like he knew he was defeated. After his years of meanness, it was a great sight.

I might have enjoyed the fun for weeks, until I made the mistake of describing it to Mom at supper that night.

She didn't say much in reply. "Be careful, Ricky. Picking on Butch isn't fair, either, and it may be even worse than what he did to you. After all, you already know from him what it's like to be bullied."

Just like parents to spoil fun.

Naturally, I couldn't forget her warning the next day at school.

Two people stomped on Butch's toes on purpose during a baseball game. Someone else stole his sandwich. And everyone else teased him as often as possible. And always, the *nyah, nyah, nenyahnyah*s.

I couldn't enjoy it as much as before, because I kept seeing things from Butch's point of view.

Later in the day I turned a corner in the hallway, bumped into Butch, and caught him with tears in his eyes.

"Go ahead, laugh some more," he said, sniffling. "Hit me with another *nyah, nyah, nenyahnyah.*"

I didn't want to feel sorry for him, but it was difficult not to.

"Nah, I get bad colds myself," I finally said. "They plug my nose and make my eyes water, too. If people didn't know better, they could think I was crying, my colds get so bad."

He grinned a little. "Yeah."

He looked so human with that sudden smile that when another thought hit me, I blurted my next words without thinking.

"Look, Butch, I got a deal for you, okay? It's going to take a couple of nights after school with me, but I think there's a way to fix that cold of yours."

He stared at me for a second, wondering what kind of trick I was going to play on him.

"Butch," I said, "no surprises. I'll explain the deal, and if you like it, we'll go ahead with it."

By the time I finished explaining, his grin had gone from little to really big.

The next few days were tough on Butch. He had been a bully for so long that people went overboard trying to make up for it now. It was so bad that before classes started, when most of us in the school hung around the swings waiting for the bell to ring, Butch would stay near the road, alone and kicking gravel against the curb. If it wasn't for our deal, he probably would've gone crazy.

Three mornings later, on the playground before classes started, I was talking to my friends Lisa Higgins, Mike Andrews, and Ralphy Zee, when Lisa looked over my shoulder, and her eyes flared wide with fear.

I turned, then understood her horror.

A monstrous dog was running toward the gap between all of us there and the safety of the school.

Ripper—Mrs. McEwan's Great Dane.

Every single one of us stopped in mid-movement. The usual laughing and shouting stilled to a silence that let us hear the drifting sounds of faraway birds.

It was a justified fear.

Mrs. McEwan's Great Dane is taller than most kids. Ripper was totally black and, just by himself, looked like an entire pack of wolves.

Most of the time Mrs. McEwan kept him behind a tall chain-link fence, and whenever anyone went by, he would throw himself against the fence, growling and barking, nearly tearing the fence out of the ground.

Now Ripper was free. And headed in a silent trot straight for us.

Then someone screamed, and all of us began to run for the safety of the slide. Ripper began to bark and to jump up and down in excitement, swinging that huge head in all directions, as if unable to decide who to chomp first.

Suddenly Butch Dolby appeared. We had been so busy worrying about the dog that we didn't notice Butch had left his lonely gravel-kicking spot at the road.

Butch ran past all of us to face the barking and slavering Great Dane. Butch put his hands out in front of him and made a command.

"Stop right there, dog," Butch said in a deep, confident voice.

Ripper barked louder, then ducked his head and bolted toward Butch. Butch kept his hands in front of his chest, as if pushing Ripper away, and didn't back away a single step.

"Beat it! Leave us alone!"

Ripper stopped as if he had rammed an invisible barrier of glass, then sat and barked softer, with hesitation.

"That's right, pal," Butch said in a more soothing tone. "Leave us alone."

Now Ripper whined at Butch. Butch stepped closer and grabbed him by the collar. "We're going home now, boy," he said to the dog.

Butch pulled on Ripper's collar and tugged him along as they left the playground in the direction of Mrs. McEwan's house. It was an amazing sight, for Ripper's head reached as high as Butch's shoulders.

I tried to hide my smile.

Because from where we were, it was impossible to see Butch feeding dog biscuits to Ripper with his other hand as they walked together in what no one else knew was friendship.

I knew both things, though. I also knew that the entire time Butch had faced Ripper, he had held his hands in front of him to show those dog biscuits.

And I also knew that barely five minutes earlier, Joel had let Ripper out of Mrs. McEwan's yard and led him to the edge of the playground. Joel, of course, in his ghostly and mysterious ways of innocence, had always been best friends with Ripper.

But then, Joel had also shared a lot of dog biscuits with Ripper.

There wasn't much to becoming friends with Ripper. All you had to do was what Joel did. Share dog biscuits. Unfortunately, you also had to do it the way that Joel did—one bite for you, and one bite for Ripper.

For Butch it had taken seven and a half boxes of dog biscuits over the last week, so many biscuits that Butch later confessed he'd begun to enjoy the taste.

When Butch returned to the school from Mrs. McEwan's yard that morning, he was the hero of us all. Nobody picked on him again. And he didn't pick on anyone, either, because when people begin to genuinely like you, it's hard to be mean in return.

There was, of course, another reason that Butch never dared pick on anyone smaller again.

Blackmail.

Butch knew he would always have a tough time explaining my photographs of him and Ripper happily sharing a snack of dog biscuits.

"Nyah, nyah, nenyahnyah":
Thoughts on *The Hero of Jamesville*

EVER TRIED SHARING a biscuit with a dog larger than yourself?

I have, but I don't remember.

Mothers, as you probably know from experience, are not allowed to graduate from their training school until they've perfected the art of telling embarrassing stories about their children, right in front of that child, and always to complete strangers to that child.

The only thing I can think of to counteract that is to have embarrassing stories about your mother to tell in return. Failing that, because mothers rarely seem to make mistakes, about the best you can do is hope to write about those embarrassing stories.

(Keep that in mind the next time your teacher plunks down a creative writing assignment. Steal your story ideas from your own childhood.)

So when I sat down in front of the computer to write *The Hero of Jamesville*, of course I remembered Mom's story (how could I forget, she's told it to so many strangers) about the time I wandered away from home and was found sitting in the middle of a faraway street sharing biscuits with a dog that was twice the size of my three-year-old body.

Nobody knows how I escaped the backyard, or how I made it that far, or where I got the biscuits. And nobody knows where I found the dog, or where it went later.

But to Mom's horror, there I was, in the center of a quiet back street, reaching upward to put the biscuit and my tiny fingers in the mouth of a dog big enough to scare her, then pulling my drool-covered hand away to take my own bite.

I often wonder about that dog—how it managed to treat me with such gentleness and patience when I was so determined to eat my fair share of our food.

And I wonder about my trust of that huge dog, about the innocence of small children.

Little kids and dogs, I've decided, because they don't have words to use as tools and weapons, communicate peace and maybe even love on a silent level the rest of us in our loudness will never be able to understand.

Yup, little kids and dogs are nice to one another.

That's something I hope to remember the next time I have the urge to hit someone hard with a *Nyah, nyah, nenyahnyah.*

CURRENT EVENTS 7

Wise people ignore Mike Andrews on hot spring Saturdays when he's busting to make up for a long winter indoors. Unfortunately, wisdom is not my strong point, especially around someone who thinks the word *impossible* means *just try harder.*

Which wouldn't be so bad, except for my other friend, Ralphy Zee. He's the computer genius type. A head full of information, most of which should have stayed in the encyclopedias he got it from.

So when they showed up Saturday morning with a roll of plastic, a sledgehammer, some fence posts, and wide planks, I should have gone back to bed. Instead, I stupidly listened to the plan.

Seconds later I decided I hadn't been so stupid.

"A fishing and swimming hole! All our own! Great idea, guys. How long do you think it'll take?"

Ralphy pulled a small memo pad from his back pocket and consulted his notes. "Hmm. Flow is minuscule—Mike, that means tiny—less than two cubic feet per second. The new structure will sustain—Mike, that means handle—a pressure per square inch of—"

"Enough, Einstein," Mike growled. "Will it fill by this afternoon?"

Ralphy grinned. "Depends how quick we build."

Mike didn't even reply. He just picked up the four wooden fence posts, the roll of plastic, and the sledgehammer and started walking. Which left Ralphy and me with the heavy wooden planks. No surprise there.

By the time we caught up to Mike, he had already pounded one fence post as far as it would go.

"Took you long enough."

I blinked sweat from my eyes and merely scowled.

"Did Joel follow?" Mike then asked.

"Dumb question, Mike. It's not like we ever know anyway." Joel's my six-year-old brother. A tiny ghost-like kid who appears when you want him least.

Mike grinned agreement, then attacked the next fence post with a fury he never devotes to schoolwork.

I looked around. "Not bad planning, Ralphy."

We were in a small ravine on the edge of our small town of Jamesville. The creek at the bottom was so small it didn't even have a name. We hoped to change that soon.

Upstream, or as Ralphy called it, *uptrickle*, the banks on each side of the creek were a stone's throw apart—with mostly dry land between—and about five feet high. But where we stood, the distance between the banks had narrowed so that our long wooden planks could reach from one side to the other.

Ralphy's suggestion had been so simple, it verged on genius. All we needed were two fence posts on each bank. It took only half an hour to set up. When we finished, there was barely an inch between the posts of each pair, one pair on the north side of the creek, one pair on the south side.

Then all we had to do was slip the wooden planks into the slots between the fenceposts, just like dropping a crossbar into place. Dropping the first wide plank in created a wall about ten inches high directly across the creek. The second plank doubled the height

of the wall. And so on. Within minutes, the wall was the height of
the fence posts.

"Okay," Ralphy said. "Start unfolding our plastic against the
wall. The force of water should hold the plastic in place, and no
water will seep through the cracks between the planks."

"No sooner said than done," Mike said with a salute.

He was right.

And we watched with admiration as the water slowly piled up
against our sturdy homemade dam.

By two that afternoon, we started to get nervous.

"Ralphy," Mike asked, "isn't this pond of ours going to stop filling?"

"Of course," he said.

"That's good," Mike said. "I was beginning to get worried."

"I just don't know when it'll stop," Ralphy finished.

"Wonderful," I said.

We stared at our swimming hole. Ralphy had picked the perfect
spot for his dam. Where it stood, the banks cut in so quickly to the
narrowed part that they, along with the dam, held much of the
weight of the water. Yet behind the dam, the banks widened so
quickly that for every inch that the water level rose, the pond grew
a foot wider.

An anxious feeling in my stomach was growing as quickly as
the water level was. Somehow, I didn't know how smart this idea
was.

It didn't take long for us to discover my trouble radar was in
good working order. And, naturally, it had to be Joel who showed
us why.

The first indication came with his usual—and as usual totally unexpected—tap on my shoulder.

"Joel," I said between gritted teeth as I landed, "when are you going to learn not to follow people? And when are you going to learn to say hello instead of scaring them to death?"

He ignored my usual lecture. "I'm sad," he said. "Will the baby birds go to heaven?"

I sighed. "What baby birds?"

He pulled his hand out from behind his back. Instead of his teddy bear, he held a tiny and fuzzy bird.

"That's not right," I began. "Leave the bird in the nest. You can't interfere with nature like—"

A sick feeling washed over me. Joel's shoes were soaked. *Where had he been?*

"Moved the nest," he said, the sadness growing. "The babies can't swim."

"The pond!" I shouted to Mike and Ralphy. "Ground-nesting birds don't have a chance!"

Then I realized there were probably hundreds of different creatures—tiny and out of sight—that we were drowning. My sick feeling inside mushroomed.

"Ralphy," I pleaded. "Think of something."

He studied the dam. "We could wiggle the fence posts free. But the dam would burst and send a flash flood. That'd be major trouble."

He thought a second more. "If we tear the plastic away, there should be enough space between the cracks of the planks for the water to escape fast without too much danger."

"Most of the plastic's underwater," Mike protested.

I began peeling away my shirt. "Tell that to Joel's bird," I said. I didn't wait for the answer but began wading into our pond. I fought the urge to scream against the cold water. Before I could chicken out, I ducked my head under, closed my eyes against the dirty water, and reached out blindly for the plastic.

I tore as much away as I could before running out of breath. I hit the surface gasping, and as I prepared to duck under again, I saw Mike and Ralphy wading in.

In a few frenzied minutes we had torn enough plastic loose so that water began pouring through the cracks.

We trudged back to shore. Immediately the edges of the pond began to recede.

"Whew," Mike said. "For once I'm glad that brother of yours made an appearance."

"Me too," I said. "Dad would call this a good lesson about messing around with the environment."

Mike and Ralphy nodded.

I brightened. "But at least there's enough time left in the afternoon for our pants to dry. With luck, we won't have to explain too much of this."

Mike and Ralphy nodded again. Mike turned to find a comfortable patch of grass to soak up the sunshine.

I giggled.

"Hey, Mike," I snorted. "We don't need my dad to teach us this lesson. Ole Mother Nature is taking care of it herself."

"What do you mean?" he said through a suspicious squint as he faced me again.

"Not much," I snorted again. "Except for the three bloodsuckers on your back."

Mike started dancing and screaming and beating his back. Ralphy spun around to look.

My snort became a full laugh. "Mother Nature dished it out on you, too, Ralphy. You've got two between your shoulder blades!"

"Eeeeyahhh!" Funny how far off the ground that skinny guy could get.

I felt a tickle just above my belt. My laugh trailed off to a dry rattle.

"Ralphy," I begged fearfully as I twisted around. "Tell me my back is clean."

"Four of them," he wailed a second later. "Big ones."

We didn't stop running or screaming until we reached home, and it still took Mom half an hour after removing them to convince us nobody ever died from vampire leeches.

CONTENTS—ONE WORLD: HANDLE WITH CARE: Thoughts on *Current Events*

I CAN'T THINK OF environmental issues without remembering the moment—at age sixteen—when I stood and shouted outrage at a middle-aged stranger. The good part was that he couldn't see me. The bad part was the reason he couldn't see me—I was live on the radio at the time.

It was a call-in talk show, and I was one of three high-school students invited to discuss the issue of whether to dam the Red Deer River. The huge concrete dam—if given government approval—would form a lake miles long and miles wide in a valley thirty miles upstream of our town of Red Deer. Regulation of water flow would then make possible the nearby location of several world-scale natural gas processing plants, each plant costing hundreds of millions of dollars to construct.

Environmental groups were rallying against the Red Deer River Dam. Public hearings took place in every community hall as the issue was debated. And our high school biology class was gathering names on petitions, protesting, and trying to do as much as possible to stop scheduled construction.

Part of our efforts included the call-in radio talk show. The three of us students were live, on air, and debating the listening public.

The show itself went smoothly. We had, of course, statistics and dire predictions showing the nightmares that would occur if the dam was actually built, and we had argument after argument much practiced and ready for this occasion.

Fifteen minutes into the show, we had answered maybe a dozen callers. Most offered reasons why it was terrible to dam the river. Then came the man who suggested perhaps progress was not such a bad thing.

That's when I exploded. I rarely lose my temper, but all our weeks and frustration seemed to be magnified in this moment, and without warning a rage boiled inside me, and I launched into a passionate, heated lecture and actually began to tell this man in a shout exactly where he could take his opinion when—

—the radio talk-show host pulled the plug on my microphone.

That's how angry I'd become. The man running the show leaned over and unplugged me, which effectively ended my short-lived radio career. But at the time I wasn't embarrassed that I had shown so little respect in front of so many people. Instead, I felt justified in my behavior, almost proud of what I'd done. After all, the environment is so tremendously important, it needed crusaders like me.

Right?

Now I don't think so. Now when I remember the episode, I don't feel proud at all.

Treating our environment with respect is very important, but approaching that issue with tempered reason and fairness is even more important. No issue, not even the extremely fashionable environmental movement, needs crusaders who are fanatics.

Because no changes can be good changes unless they involve reasoned thought and fairness.

The Oxford dictionary defines a fanatic as "a person filled with excessive and often misguided enthusiasm for something." Someone else once described a fanatic as someone who redoubles his efforts when he loses sight of his goal. Fanatics are the type of people who blow up cars in crowded streets, simply to prove a point. Fanatics are the type of people who start religious wars that kill thousands, all in their efforts to promote a God of love. In short, fanatics use any means possible and justify themselves by pointing to the goal they are trying to achieve.

Unfortunately, on the anti-dam crusade, I verged on being fanatic. Not once, not even for a moment, would I allow myself or anyone I debated a chance to consider the other side of the issue. And there were valid points to consider.

A dam would reduce yearly major spring flood damage. A dam would produce cheap electricity without the dangers of nuclear power, without the noxious smoke of burning coal. A dam—and the environmentally clean natural gas processing plants—would provide hundreds of jobs. Those jobs, in turn, would support hundreds of families, giving thousands of people the chance to live and dream and love with real financial security.

Yes, there were very good reasons to support either side of the issue, and I am disappointed in myself for not having had the wisdom to realize that.

Perhaps, after weighing all the pros and cons, I would still have been able to reasonably and intelligently support the anti-dam side. Or perhaps instead I would have realized that yes, we needed to build a dam. But either way, my decision would have then been based on an open-minded review of all the facts, not simply the ones I wanted to hear.

I now believe your internal warning sirens should grow louder the more right you believe you are. The time to listen most closely to the other side is the time when you passionately think you are most right, because that is the time you are most likely to be blinded to the situation as it is. If you truly are right, then your opinion will survive any test. If you are wrong, however, by considering the other side, you will be taking the best moment possible to give the voice of reason a chance to temper your views.

I still feel the same way about environmental issues as I did then in high school. We must handle our world with care. I hope that's reflected in *Current Events*. Mike, Ricky, and Ralphy did not reason out the consequences of their actions before building *their* dam, and that, of course, led to the small-scale environmental disaster that they faced.

In the same way, environmental crusaders can and should raise battle cries against any foes who do not carefully weigh the results of building a factory, a dam, or clearing land.

Yet—and I am sure my reservations arise from the regret of the total single-mindedness of my own anti-dam work—I believe it is not realistic to expect that we can let nature be an untended garden, free from human interference.

For us to eat, fields must be cleared and livestock raised. To maintain hospitals, electricity must be produced. To stay warm, we must build houses. And so the list continues.

I believe, then, we should be as much afraid of the environmentalist zealots who would have all of us living in log cabins as we need fear those who would burrow, burn, trample, and poison God's earth in pursuit of profit.

The difficult part is to find ways to sustain us without destroying the very world that sustains us. Finding that path, of course, arises only from applying reason and fairness.

The Red Deer River Dam?

It was built a few years after I had graduated from high school.

The environmentalists who lost the battle will say that the government and corporate people in power had planned to build the dam all along, that the public hearings were held simply to make it appear as if those affected by the dam would have a say in the matter.

Others might say, instead, that the vocal environmentalists were simply a loud minority, and that the majority of people did not care whether the dam was built.

Still others might say that after years of studies—economic and environmental—a painful decision was made, one that considered all the pros and cons and decided that for a small environmental loss in one area, the environment and economic gains made the building of the dam a reasonable choice.

It is my hope and thought that the third opinion is closer to the truth.

Of course, that huge concrete structure upstream of Red Deer is still not a favorite on my list.

Sure, behind it is a new lake, one which gives thousands of people pleasure, one which now holds an entirely new world of aquatic wildlife. Sure, the river no longer rips and tears and floods each spring. Sure, the natural gas processing plants with all their finely tuned environmental controls now provide hundreds of jobs.

None of that matters to me when it comes to the Red Deer River Dam.

I don't like it for a simple reason. Last summer I spent eight hours fishing at the base of that dam. Men, women, and children all around me caught shining trout. Me? Not a thing.

Maybe I should have been gentler about the dam on the radio.

THE FIGHT 8

Nobody past the age of two should ever be involved in a fight over a teddy bear. That's what I told myself as I began to sprint across the playground. Nobody.

But then, few people have a younger brother like Joel, who insists on owning that teddy bear. And fewer are at bat during recess to notice after a big swing and miss that Randy Temples has taken the teddy bear away from Joel.

I dropped my bat and stared.

Then Randy Temples threw the teddy bear high and kicked it on its way down.

That's when I began to sprint.

Actually, there must have been a thousand times when I wanted to strangle Joel's dumb teddy bear myself, but brothers are allowed to do that. When I'm mad at Joel, I remind him that teddy bear stuffing is hard to replace. It gets his attention. But just like all the other threats toward Joel that I mutter beneath my breath, I know deep down I'm only bluffing.

Now, to see the bewildered hurt on Joel's face, I wondered if I could ever even make that threat again. It was an expression that made me white-hot angry inside. Randy Temples was big, mean, and ugly, but I guess since I was crazy enough to fight over a teddy bear, I was crazy enough not to be scared.

He saw me coming.

He held the teddy bear away from him like he dared me to grab it. What he didn't know was that by now the teddy bear was the last thing on my mind. I didn't veer half a step as I buried my head and slammed him directly in the center of his chest.

He was as surprised as I was. We fell over together. I got up first and took the teddy bear from the ground and tossed it to Joel. Then, as my anger faded, I worried about Randy Temples.

His eyes were popping with madness. He put up his fists. I did, too, not that I knew much about fighting.

"You're going to get yours," he said.

"Just leave my brother and his bear alone," I panted.

He moved toward me. It was hard not to move back.

Then the bell rang for everyone to come in for classes.

He put his fists down. In front of everybody watching, he said, "Tonight after school you better come back here to finish this off."

I nodded.

Then he stopped and looked a little embarrassed. "I forgot. I have a doctor's appointment tonight. The fight will be tomorrow after school."

I was glad we were in different classes so that he couldn't see how nervous I was for the rest of the day.

At suppertime I couldn't eat much, and my dad didn't take long to notice.

"What's up, Ricky? You're nearly as quiet as Joel tonight."

"Nothing," I said.

"Mmmph."

I would have been off the hook, too, except for Joel. We had

Jell-O with whipped cream for dessert, one of his favorites. And he didn't gobble it down with a lot of noise like usual. Instead, he took the bowl, carried it around to my side of the table, and patted my head. That meant *thank you*. Then he disappeared.

Dad looked at Mom.

"Okay, Ricky, spill the beans," Dad said.

So I told him everything.

"You know I don't believe in fighting," he said.

"But, Dad, asking Randy Temples nicely sure wouldn't have helped. Besides, he has to know he can't pick on Joel and get away with it."

He became thoughtful. "You will need a lot of strength," he said.

"I know. Randy Temples has the biggest muscles in school."

He said something very strange. "No, son, if that kind of strength mattered, really mattered, it would be a sad world."

I just wanted advice on how to punch. I would need it.

He smiled sadly. "I'm not helping you much, am I?"

I shook my head.

Then he grinned. "Okay. We'll try it my way first. Then I'll help you on yours."

Dad's way didn't seem to be much of a help. It meant a long discussion on the definition of courage, the stupidity of violence, and references to wise men and women in the past who found other solutions instead of fighting.

With that kind of attitude, I knew I'd be slaughtered after school. I looked for a way to at least be allowed one punch. I said, "Speaking of history, wouldn't you say King David was a wise man?"

Dad saw that one coming. He started to put up his hands in protest, but I pushed on.

"And didn't David kill Goliath?"

"Yes, but—" Dad tried to protest.

"Then grabbed Goliath's sword and chopped off his head?"

"Yes, but—"

"And carried the head around so everyone could see?" I quickly said. "Dripping blood and all—"

"All right, all right, all right! You made your point."

"Great," I said. "You give me a quick course in boxing? I promise not to chop Randy Temples' head off and—"

"I did promise you we'd try it your way, didn't I," he interrupted. His voice then became thoughtful. "Remember this, though, Ricky. King David first had strength inside and the wisdom to know when he really had to fight."

Then his face lit up in a grin. "Now let's discuss how we'll do it your way if it becomes necessary."

Naturally, everybody at school knew about the upcoming fight between me and Randy Temples after school.

Mike asked me if he could have my comic books while I was in the hospital. Questions like that don't help your frame of mind.

Before I knew it, school was over for the day. I walked slowly over to the baseball diamond. Randy Temples was there with a mean look on his face. All his friends and all my friends were there; so was nearly everyone else.

He took off his jacket. So did I. I had on my heaviest and loosest sweater.

He put up his fists.

I didn't.

"Fight," he said.

I shook my head. "I want you to leave my brother alone. And I think fighting is a dumb way to do this."

He sneered and his friends laughed. "You're chicken," he said. "I knew it."

"No, I'm not chicken." I tried the logic that my dad had used on me. "Fighting only proves one of us is a better fighter than the other. And just because you're a better fighter doesn't mean you're right."

With everyone watching, it was still pretty quiet.

"Nice try, chicken." To his friends, he said, "Let's go, guys, I can't stand cowards."

"Stay," I said. "Nobody here is a coward." I pointed to my stomach. "Hit me."

"What?"

"Hit me. If you think you are proving something by fighting, go ahead. Hit me. I'm not scared of you. I just won't fight back."

He grinned. "Great. Watch this, guys. I'll hit him so hard he'll get picked up for speeding."

He moved real close to me. His breathing was heavy.

I put my hands on my hips to give him my whole stomach to punch.

Over his shoulder he said, "I'll hit him so hard, his mama will fall down."

He brought his fist back to swing. I tried not to flinch.

Then he swung. I didn't move to protect myself.

Nothing happened. He had missed on purpose.

There was disbelief on his face that I would just let him take his hardest swing at me.

"You mean it, don't you," he said. "You won't run away, but you won't fight back. Are you crazy?"

"No," I said. "I think I'm right, though. That makes it easier."

He brought his fist back again and studied my face. I was prepared to let him swing.

"Aw, forget it," he said. "I don't care if your dumb brother marries that teddy bear."

After that he didn't bother me or Joel much. In fact, he even became my friend later. But I never told him how badly he would have hurt himself by swinging that day.

Because when I got home that night, Dad asked, "Did you learn something about the strength of courage today?"

I nodded. "He didn't hit me."

Dad said, "Good. It's a tough lesson. I hope you can remember it when you need to show wisdom again." He grinned. "Next time you might not be wearing your backup plan."

I grinned back and took off my loose and bulky sweater.

Dad helped me remove the backup plan that I wore underneath. It was a square piece of board that we had strapped for protection across my stomach in the morning before I went to school. After all, as Dad had reminded me, King David used the smartest way possible whenever he actually *had* to fight.

SWING, DUCK, OR RUN AWAY:
Thoughts on *The Fight*

P ROBABLY AT ANY AGE, and especially any age under fourteen, there are two components of worry when someone challenges you to a fistfight.

The first worry, of course, is how not to get hurt. Five bony knuckles smashing into your nose is not exactly a day brightener.

The second worry is just as bad—the consequences. And for kids, chances are after any fight—win, lose, or draw—there will be adults to face afterward, adults who won't appear happy with anything as childish as a fistfight, no matter who started it.

Unfortunately, adult theories, advice, and principles don't do much good when some guy is breathing in your face and daring you to fight.

Because it's not like you can hold up an index finger right at that moment and say, "Excuse me. Did you know that the principle of nonviolent resistance served Mahatma Gandhi so well that his campaigns were the most important factor leading to the British withdrawal from India in 1947?"

Also, no matter how good the advice sounds at the supper table the night before, it just doesn't work to walk away declaring, "This is me with my head held high because my mommy says there is nothing cowardly about avoiding a fight." Chances are you'll really get picked on in the future because kids believe you're a coward; worse, you might actually begin to believe it yourself.

And you'll never calm down your opponent with this statement: "I'd really like to fight, but my father says that only stupid people use violence to achieve their goals. So I guess that means you're stupid."

Nope. Nope. And nope. Adult theories, advice, and principles don't do much good when some guy is breathing in your face and daring you to fight.

A big part of that problem, it seems to me, is the difference between a kids' world and the one of grown-ups.

Adults rarely engage in fistfights. We're older and more sophisticated, and we've learned to fight with nastier methods—insults (the subtler the better), rumors, through the power of money and status. Not only is it not considered cool to punch someone's lights out, there is a real threat any fistfight would lead to criminal charges. Generally, in the adult world, it's not part of the rules to expect fistfights to solve or win anything.

On the other hand, in a kids' world, the rules are different. Sure, in calm discussion most everyone in your class will agree that the truth is simple—fighting is wrong. On a moral level, fighting— physically or by any other method—*is* wrong. People should not try to hurt other people.

But what *should* happen and what *does* happen are two different things. Not only do fistfights happen with frequency in school, fistfights generally have great significance. As anyone still in school knows too well, the toughest kids are rewarded for their toughness; "wimps" lose out.

In short, if ever you're challenged to a fight in school, you're in a no-win situation. Victory in *your* world—proving toughness by fighting well—means a defeat in the adult world, a defeat often accompanied by punishment. But victory in an adult sense—walking away, seeking compromise—too often means defeat in your school world.

To complicate it more, some adults do use violence as an outlet, or to deliver punishment. The lashing out rarely happens in public, but in the home. And in these homes, it is very difficult for kids not to learn to use violence themselves when they are outside of the home.

These kids, at school, have no problem breaking the adult rules against fighting. What do you do when someone like that uses fighting as a solution? Especially when it seems the only way to stop violence is with violence.

What to do when challenged with a fight?

Ricky Kidd, of course, in *The Fight*, found a solution that managed to work for both worlds; he maintained honor without fighting. It was a lot easier, however, to arrange that in fiction than in real life—I, for one, never got into the habit of wearing protective wood under my clothing each day I went to school.

What to do when challenged with a fight?

I think it's a much more important question than some adults realize. When school is the biggest part of your daily life, and when some kids at school see fighting as a method to get their way or to prove themselves, to fight or not to fight becomes an inevitable decision because there will be the inevitable challenge, and one with bigger consequences than might appear on the surface. Life is miserable for someone who chooses to believe he or she is a coward, and no matter what adults say, it feels cowardly to back away.

What to do when challenged with a fight?

I'd be crazy to try to answer, for I have no right to pretend to be the authority on the question. I also have no right to presume whatever answer I might offer is correct. And lastly, this definitely is an issue to be discussed with the adults in your own life.

Maybe, then, the thoughts that led to writing *The Fight* might be a starting point for those discussions. For example, in any discussion, I hope that it's worthwhile to consider the "adult rules and kids' rules" on fighting and the practical difficulties caused by those different perspectives.

After that?

In the story *The Fight*, I think I was trying to tell Ricky Kidd this: One, learn the difference between an avoidable fight and an unavoidable fight; two, if you have to fight, protect yourself as well as possible.

Which leads to the million-dollar question: What's an avoidable fight? Most, I believe, are. A lot of times a good joke can break the tension, or an offered compromise. It never hurts to try either, especially if the other person is as nervous about fighting as you are.

Sometimes, however, the other person is determined to fight or is already swinging and there is no time for words. What then?

There's something strange about fighting, something I think mothers sometimes forget. Even if you lose, you gain respect for not running away, and chances are you won't have to fight again. In other words, you don't have to win the fight to be a winner; you don't have to hurt the other person for the fight to end.

On a theoretical level, it's known as passive resistance. Martin Luther King Jr., who was determined to change racial prejudice in the 1960s, often faced violence as he fought for civil rights, yet he did not resort to violent tactics in return. Mahatma Gandhi, the great leader of India, was able to persuade his people to resist violence with nonviolent tactics. (Once he and a crowd, instead of fighting, actually lay down in front of British soldiers mounted on horses. The tactic worked, for the horses refused to advance, and the soldiers could not shoot people who weren't armed.)

While passive resistance sounds like an excellent theory, how does it work at a school level where no one cares about King or Gandhi and where specific people are very interested in causing blood to run down your face?

I would tell Ricky that on a practical level—when the fight absolutely can't be avoided—that people should protect themselves as well as possible. For example, if you're big enough, you can wrestle the other person into a stalemate. You're not exactly fighting, but you're not running away, either. If you're quick enough, you can hold your ground and duck most of the action. If you fit neither category, make fists and get your hands up in front of your face. Most of the punches will bounce off your forearms and elbow and shoulders, and the other person will tire out. Professional boxers often use this tactic.

I'd really like to stress that my advice to Ricky Kidd is simply *my* advice. My background and experience has led me to believe that running away from an unavoidable fight is worse in the long-term than standing your ground and protecting yourself; there are others whose background has led them to decide that violence must be avoided at all costs.

And yup, giving advice is a lot easier than taking it. At age seventeen, I had a fight in hockey that was a perfect example of what not to do.

For starters, it was an avoidable fight. When the guy ran me over and fell to the ice beside me, I could have skated away. I'd been concentrating on hockey all season and had skated away from worse cheap shots.

But already we'd played thirty games, I was the only guy on the team who hadn't been in a fight, and, when I was honest with myself, I had to wonder if I *was* afraid of the physical side of hockey. So I took a lot of abuse.

Until this time.

I'd had enough. I got to my feet first and punched the guy in the head as he was rising. Not because I needed to protect myself. But because I had to prove something to me and to the others on the team.

Dumb.

I was punished immediately for that mistake, because when the guy got to his feet, I found myself looking upward at his face. He was that big.

Unfortunately, I couldn't back down, not after starting the stupid thing.

In hockey, it's traditional that both fighters throw off their gloves before swinging away at each other.

Did I mention this was my first hockey fight?

I made fists with each hand and then tried to throw my gloves off.

See for yourself what that leads to. Put a glove or mitt on, make a fist, keep the fist, and then try to shake the glove off. No way. It stays on your hand for as long as you're making a fist.

In the heat of the fight, I was too flustered to realize that.

I kept my fists clenched and kept trying to throw my gloves off, but it was like trying to shake a pair of terriers loose from my sleeves. And the entire time I was concentrating on getting my gloves off, this big guy—who'd easily slipped his own gloves onto the ice—was raining punches all over my face.

Avoid the fight if you can, and if a fight is absolutely necessary, protect yourself as well as possible.

I lost on both counts; the blood I blew from my nose all over the sink in the dressing room proved it.

If only I could have figured out a way to rig some protection beneath my sweater before the game—

Normally, a person would think it strange to see his best friend and roommate insist on sleeping with a baseball bat. But this was no ordinary baseball bat. And Mike Andrews—in the middle of a feud that had grown too big—was taking no chances.

"Did you see the way Haywood made a grab for this in the locker room after the game?" Mike whispered in the darkness. "Four generations of family baseball, and he wants to mess with it." Mike paused long enough to snort. "That'll be the day."

Haywood meant Luke Haywood. New kid in the class one month earlier and a last-minute addition to the school baseball team. Breaking in like that would have been tough enough without doing something stupid on the first day he met Mike Andrews, our team captain.

"How ya doing?" Luke Haywood had asked that afternoon on the baseball diamond.

"Fine." Mike's lips had been saying one thing. His eyes were saying another as they scanned the new kid up and down in obvious examination of baseball potential.

He saw what the rest of us did. A kid of average height, slightly curly hair, a gap between his two front teeth, and a hand extended as he waited for Mike to shake his hand.

Mike shrugged and took his hand. Then yelled and jumped and howled for ten seconds.

"Joy buzzer," Luke grinned, then looked to us on the rest of the team to see how much we had appreciated the joke.

"Idiot," Mike replied without a return grin as he sucked air between his teeth, then stomped away to leave Luke alone at the backstop as the rest of us followed our team captain to our practice positions in the field.

It wasn't a great start for Luke, even if, as our skinny friend Ralphy pointed out, Mike would have been happy to do the same thing if he'd have thought of it first. Mike—red hair, Hawaiian shirt, and mismatched sneakers—lives to play jokes on other people.

As if to compensate for losing round one, Mike had spent a lot of time in the next four weeks in extra effort to make Luke's life miserable. We had helped, too. After all, Mike was our friend.

There were the standard tricks. A snake in Luke's desk. Salt shaker unscrewed in the lunchroom just before it reached Luke. Honey in his baseball glove after school. Even itching powder in his uniform before a game.

Unfortunately, Luke didn't seem to get the message. Ralphy walked from the bench during the seventh inning of one game to bat, and fell flat on his face in front of all the spectators—Luke had tied his shoes together. I handed in a six-page report and then had to try to explain to the entire class while Luke smirked from the back row why pages two through six had only one line—*teacher smells*—repeated again and again. Mike found one small dead frog in each of his baseball shoes—the hard way.

More unfortunately, Luke Haywood played great baseball. Enough so that the other guys on the team—who neither inflicted nor were inflicted in return with jokes—decided he was an all right guy.

And now, out of town overnight and trying to fall asleep in our hotel room only twelve hours away from the championship game, Mike was almost regretting what he had started.

It was in the tone of his voice. "He can't touch the bat," Mike said. "I'll guard it with my life. Especially if we win."

Especially if we win meant he would be able to add his signature to the old wooden bat. The bat had been in Mike's family for four generations, over sixty-five years. Every time someone in the Andrews' family was part of a championship team, that player signed it. Twenty years had passed since its last signature. If we won tomorrow, Mike could sign it right along with the greatest players in his family history, alongside his grandfather and some uncles and a cousin who had made it into the majors for half a season.

"Mike," Ralphy whispered from the other side of the room, "it might be a good time to ease up on the new guy. He *is* part of our team, and tomorrow's a big game. Plus, you won't have to worry about your bat."

Fake snores answered him in the darkness—Mike's way of saying *Not a chance, pal.*

We had a 2–0 lead at the end of the third inning. Mike had taken the bat into the showers with him before the game started.

It was tied at 3 with two innings left. Mike had made the coach pledge to guard the bat while he was out in the field.

Mike hit a double in the eighth, and Luke singled him home to give us a 4–3 lead. But instead of jumping with the rest of the team and showing joy, Mike had carefully checked the family bat to make sure it was still untouched.

We shut them down the rest of the game to win. Mike made very sure he was holding his precious bat as the rest of us whooped and shouted and hugged one another and celebrated.

Later we all watched gravely in the locker room as Mike

continued a long tradition and signed his family's bat.

"Thanks, guys," he grinned when he finished. "You don't know how much this means to me."

"I can only imagine," Luke said from a nearby bench. "Any chance I can look at the bat?"

The entire team laughed. By now their feud was well known.

"No chance at all," Mike said firmly but with a half grin. "I don't know what you have in mind, but if it's nearly as dangerous as you were in the game, I don't want to find out."

That compliment was as close as Mike could come to saying thanks to Luke for the game-winning RBI. The rest of us laughed again.

Luke shrugged. "No problem," he said, "but it's a long bus ride home, isn't it?"

Mike simply clutched his bat to his body for a reply.

The bat never got more than four inches away from him the entire 120 miles home. We stopped at a restaurant. Mike brought the bat in with him and spent every second inside watching Luke's every move. We made three rest room stops. Mike kept the bat with him each visit. Some of us fell asleep. Not Mike. He clutched the bat between his legs and sat with his back to the window and kept a constant eye on Luke.

And finally we reached Jamesville.

"Hah," Mike crowed as the bus pulled to a stop. "One family bat, delivered safe and sound."

Luke simply smiled.

Outside the bus a small crowd of people waited. Parents, sisters, brothers, friends. It was a nice Saturday afternoon, and it wasn't often a Jamesville team did so well.

In fact, even fat Mayor Thorpe was there to meet us, waving frantically as we stood up and gathered our gear inside the bus.

"Line up outside," our coach barked. "Mayor Thorpe wants to congratulate you guys."

We lined up. Even then, Mike refused to let go of his bat.

Mayor Thorpe had to reach his pudgy hands around the belly that bulged against his pinstriped suit, but he was determined to shake all our hands amid the applause of the small crowd.

He reached Luke Haywood. Only Mike, then I were left at the end of the line.

"Good job," Mayor Thorpe said to Luke. "I heard you drove in the winning run. It means a lot to us in a small town like this. Glad you could be part of the team."

Luke smiled modestly. "Couldn't have done it without Mike, our team captain. After all, his eighth-inning double made it possible."

Mayor Thorpe's eyes shifted to Mike. "Team captain of a championship team. Another signature to the bat I've heard so much about, even when I was growing up here. What an honor it is to—"

Luke interrupted before Mayor Thorpe could shake Mike's hand.

"Sir," Luke began.

"Yes?" Mayor Thorpe asked.

All eyes were upon us.

"Well, sir," Luke said. "Mike and I were discussing this on the way here, how much it might mean to win the game. And Mike said . . . well, I thought it was real generous of him . . . but Mike said he was going to give you that family bat to honor this occasion."

Mayor Thorpe clapped his hands together. "The Andrews bat! What a grand gesture! I'll see it hangs on the wall of the mayor's office. Mike Andrews, thank you very much!"

All eyes were still upon us. How Luke Haywood kept a straight face is beyond me. Mike was too shocked to react. And when Mayor Thorpe shook Mike's hand and took the bat, Mike was still too stunned to say anything.

"Look at all these signatures," Mayor Thorpe crooned as he cradled the bat. "Some of Jamesville's best players over the last eighty years!"

Mayor Thorpe was so excited about getting the bat that he forgot to shake my hand. He just walked away.

At our end of the line, there was frozen silence. The rest of the team scattered to rejoin parents and friends. But Mike was still rooted. Without his bat.

It took me about ten seconds. Then I began to choke on the laughter I was trying to hold back.

"I can't believe it," Mike said. "I just can't believe it. Haywood got me."

Mayor Thorpe was showing the bat to admiring friends. Mike's mom was looking in our direction in confusion. And Luke was tip-toeing away from Mike and me.

The first burst of laughter left my lips. Mike glared at me, then finally saw the humor. He giggled once and that set me off. By the time we finished laughing, we were sitting on the ground, holding our stomachs in pain.

"Haywood," Mike finally managed to shout. "Get back here!"

"Mike," I moaned, "don't you think enough is enough?"

"Hardly," Mike said as Haywood headed in our direction. "We'll need someone that smart for a friend. How else are we going to get that bat back into my family again?"

THE ACHE TO BELONG:
Thoughts on *The Baseball Feud*

HAVE YOU EVER FELT like an outsider?

My first day of school, my mother dressed me in a little suit and sent me along with a briefcase.

Before you laugh, remember that she and I had no way of knowing this was strange. I was the oldest in the family and, thus, the first one to be sent to school. Neither of us had had any practice at the first day of school.

My mother, of course, was remembering her school days in Holland, the country she had left barely seven years earlier. When *she* went to school in Europe, only the coolest kids had briefcases. And everyone dressed as formally as possible.

Not in Red Deer, Alberta, four thousand miles and twenty years away from the small village school she had attended in Holland. Briefcases and a suit in this prairie town were not part of the dress code.

It took less than three days for me to abandon the briefcase. But *Sigmund*—another gift from my immigrant background—was not a usual name. Later I skipped a grade and left all of my friends behind. And so on.

In other words, I was not natural "insider" material, not as a bookworm among older and bigger kids whose own parents spoke English without an accent.

Those memories came back to me as I was writing *The Baseball Feud*.

Insiders against outsiders.

Mike is captain of the baseball team, Ricky is his best friend, and they've known the rest of the guys for probably years. They're all part of the "inside" group.

Luke Haywood, though, the new kid on the block, tried to make friends his first day by playing a joke. It backfired and resulted in a feud between him and the "insiders."

I sympathized with Luke from the beginning on this one.

And I would be disappointed in Ricky and Mike for making it difficult for the new kid to belong, except it's a fact that friendships and loyalties by their very nature tend to lead to that kind of reaction to newcomers. Friendships and loyalties lead to groups, and a group, to exist, has to be "inside" the "outside."

That's probably true of just about every aspect of our society—kids to adults. Think of your school now. There are the nerds, the jocks, and more. There are no formal labels for each group, and perhaps the adults around you would be totally unable to identify the groups or who belongs to the groups. But you know. As does every other kid in the school.

It's no different in the adult world. Whatever the organization, small groups of friends or allies form in corporations, hospitals, political parties, or even churches. Sometimes these groups form through genuine friendship, other times because of the advantages of "knowing" a certain person. For whatever reason, these invisible groups form, just as yours do in school. Each of these "rings" are attached in various ways to other "rings" within that organization. These rings in turn are linked again to rings from other like organizations—corporation to corporation, church to church, political group to political group.

Our entire society is composed of invisible rings of "insiders" and the connections that result from these rings. The only way to ever rid ourselves of the drawbacks of "insiders" is to somehow erase from human nature the benefits of qualities like friendship and loyalty.

"Insiders" are a fact of life.

Within human nature, too, there can be no denying the fact that all of us have a deep need to belong.

That's where the troubles lie; rings exist, and we want to belong.

Luke Haywood wanted to belong. That's why he tried—perhaps too hard—with the joy buzzer joke that backfired on him.

Trying too hard leads to the danger of the small compromises that you make to belong to a certain group. A small puff of a cigarette, the puff that you don't dare decline because it might put you on the outside again, may be only the first of a series of small steps you take in a direction away from what you believe. Then, much later, you might have the regret of looking back and wondering how you managed to go so far, so badly.

I think the simplest way around falling into the trap of seeking to become an insider is to question your motives for being part of a group.

Wanting to belong simply for the sake of belonging is the time of greatest danger. It's the time when you will discover that you aren't being true to yourself—after all, you are imposing the standards of that group upon yourself. And, ironically, it's the time when you have to work the hardest to belong.

On the other hand, if you do the things you like to do, and make friendships with the friends you like, the situation is reversed. You and your true friends are imposing *your* standards on the group you form.

Maybe the best way of explaining it is to look at two people in high school.

Susan thinks musicians are cool, so she spends a lot of time trying to do whatever they do, just to be a part of the school rock band and their friends.

Tom, on the other hand, loves playing guitar. He doesn't smoke cigarettes or party when practice is over, he's just there for the music. The real musicians in that group respect him and get along with him; they don't care what he does or doesn't do away from the music.

Susan? She's not there because of a love of music; the only respect she gets or thinks she gets is by doing what she thinks musicians want her to do, which are often things she doesn't like. If Susan was really doing what she wanted, she might find herself with a totally different group of friends, a group where she feels at ease.

Another danger of trying to join a ring, I believe, is the abuse of friendship. To join the "cool" group, you may try to convince yourself that you actually enjoy the friendship of someone in that group, even if he or she has none of the kindness, humor, and loyalty of a true but less cool friend you are leaving behind.

In terms of *The Baseball Feud*, much as I often felt like an outsider growing up, I understand Ricky and Mike and Ralphy for their insider ring. They are friends, not together for the sake of being cool, not together for being part of the right group. They can't help but be insiders for one another.

If a well-meaning adult—me, the writer—had tried to force them to accept Luke Haywood, they either would have been resentful or the story would not have seemed natural.

I was glad to discover at the end—and I had no idea it would happen until I began to write the final paragraph—that they did accept Luke. Not because they were told to, but because Luke had become a true insider by earning their respect and affection.

And that, I believe, is the key. Follow your own inner voice and do what you know is right, pursue areas of life that give you pleasure, be true to yourself, and gradually you will discover that you do belong to the group that has slowly formed around you.

BLINDSIDED 10

Guys like Ernie Millhouse should be dropped into a leaky rowboat in the middle of an ocean typhoon. At least that's what my friend Mike said the day Ernie rearranged the desks of our classroom.

I had to agree.

Ernie didn't rearrange the desks by much. He must have arrived early that morning and moved them only four or five inches. Some of the rows to the left. Some of the rows to the right. A few of them ahead. A few of them back.

He moved them so little that most of us didn't even notice as we filed into the room after the buzzer rang for nine-o'clock classes and waited for the teacher to arrive.

Unfortunately, Robert Johnson didn't notice, either. At least not until he tripped over the first desk in his way.

He fell hard to the cold floor. Glasses flew in one direction. Books in another. But because it was Robert sprawled out, no giggles broke the shocked silence.

Two girls rushed over to help Robert up and brush his clothes of dirt, but having to get help probably made it worse. I picked up his dark glasses, which had skittered to my desk, and brought them back to him.

"Need a guide back to your desk?" I whispered.

"Nope." He looked somewhere past my shoulder as he

gave me a tight, brave smile. "It's my fault. Must have messed up with my mind map."

Mind map.

That's what he called it. Mind map. Robert lost his eyesight in an accident a few years ago. So now he navigated by memory. Three steps from his light switch to the bed. Twenty steps from his house to the sidewalk. Fifty-five steps to the corner. Every single room, every single path he took, he measured step by careful step.

Of course, he had a Seeing Eye dog that waited in the hallway during classes and helped Robert whenever he needed to go new places. But in familiar places, Robert always used his mind map.

His tight smile as he looked past my shoulder showed clearly that he was furious at himself for making a mistake. Worse, on the way to his desk, he stumbled over others he had never bumped into before.

That was unusual. In fact, Mike and I were always amazed at the way Robert navigated through his darkness by using those mind maps.

Except as I walked back to my desk, I noticed four tiny circles imbedded in the old wax of the tiled floor. For a second I wondered why. Then it hit me as I added the facts together. My desk had been moved. Those tiny circles were the marks from the bottom of my desk legs.

Then it hit me.

Desk moved. Robert's mind map not working.

And I caught Ernie Millhouse's smirk.

Ernie noticed me noticing, and his smirk grew.

Ernie Millhouse had moved everything just enough to make life difficult on the one person who wouldn't see the difference.

About the time I managed to stop gaping in disbelief at his cruel joke, the teacher walked in, and I had to save my accusation until class was over.

"You're a jerk, Ernie," I said when I finally caught up to him just outside the cafeteria at lunchtime. "No other way to describe it."

He snorted. "What's the matter with a little fun?"

That's when I had to intercept Mike. His red hair and ability to find trouble means he'll probably never have a career as a diplomat.

"Easy, Mike. Punching this guy's lights out won't help."

"How about an apology," Mike demanded.

Ernie snorted again. "To a blind bat?"

"Hold me back; I've changed my mind about violence," I told Mike.

Ernie just smirked, as usual.

Right then Robert reached the doorway, going slowly with his cane extended. He recognized us by our voices.

"Ricky. Mike. Ernie. How's it going, guys?"

Ernie's smirk broke into a nasty giggle. "Fine. Just fine." Then Ernie quickly stepped sideways so that when Robert spoke back, he would speak to empty air.

"Sorry for wrecking class this morning," Robert said.

"No problem," Ernie said from an unexpected side three steps over.

Robert jumped a bit, swiveled his head to face Ernie, then smiled his tight smile. "Good one, Ernie."

"You don't know the half of it," Mike said.

"Go ahead," Ernie said with mean sarcasm, "fight the bat's battles."

Robert opened his mouth to ask the obvious question, but I broke in as a great thought mushroomed in the back of my mind.

"I'll explain later," I told Robert. "But right now I have a proposition for Ernie."

Ernie and Mike gaped at the sudden change of subject. Robert simply waited with his usual patience.

"You guys know that card game called 'Go Fish?'" I asked. "Where you ask the other person for a card and try to make pairs?"

All three nodded.

"I think," I continued, "that Robert could beat Ernie two games out of three. I'm so sure of it that if Robert loses, I promise to cut the lawn for Ernie at his house all summer."

Out came Ernie's irritating smirk. "I like this so far," he said.

"But if Ernie loses," I said, "he carries around Robert's books for the rest of the school year."

"I don't understand what this is about," Robert protested.

"You will when I explain what happened to your mind map this morning," I said.

"But it wouldn't be fair for—"

"Someone as blind as a bat?" Ernie finished for Robert.

Robert's tight smile became a thin line. "I was going to say it wouldn't be fair for Ricky to be punished if I lose."

"I've got my reasons," I said. "The main one is Ernie's attitude."

Mike waved for attention. "Time out. All Ernie's got to do is look at the cards as he deals!"

Robert scowled. "I may be blind, but I'm not handicapped. The deal is on."

Ernie laughed every step he took down the hallway as he left.

Most of the class stayed after school to watch the "Go Fish" game in the back of the room. Of course, most of the class knew by then about the desk moving incident.

Ernie didn't care. He also didn't care that we saw as he looked at every one of Robert's cards—from the special Braille deck kept in the class—as he dealt them.

Someone tried protesting. After all, now Ernie knew what was in Robert's hand. It'd be easy for him to fish for pairs.

Robert said in a quiet, cold voice that reduced all of us to silence, "I don't need help. I *am* a person, you know. Not an object of pity."

Ernie just smirked and asked for a card he knew Robert had. Ernie looked at every single replacement card that he dealt to Robert and had little trouble making pairs. Ernie made a few mistakes in asking for matching cards because he couldn't remember everything he had dealt to Robert, but eventually he won that hand as dealer.

Then Robert dealt. It was like he could read Ernie's mind. Not once did he make a mistake. Within minutes, Robert had double the amount of pairs that Ernie did, and that hand was over.

"One win each," I announced. "But Robert won the second round by much more than Ernie won the first. By the rules we established, that means Robert deals again."

During the third round, Ernie even walked around the table— three times—to look over Robert's shoulders and discover exactly what he held in his hand of cards.

It didn't help.

With uncanny accuracy, Robert asked for every one of Ernie's cards that he needed, and as he finished dealing the deck, it was obvious Ernie had been slaughtered.

He threw his cards down in disgust.

"Tomorrow," I reminded him. "You'll be carrying Robert's books. And the entire school will know why."

I wasn't surprised to notice the smirk had permanently disappeared. Ernie sulked out of the room.

Later, when the rest of the class had left, Mike turned to Robert and me.

" 'Fess up, guys," he said. "How did you manage that?"

"We blindsided him," I said. "Caught him from an angle he couldn't see."

Robert chuckled. "I like that. Blindsided. I suppose he deserved it, didn't he?"

I nodded, then quickly said yes as I remembered Robert could not see my head move. "By the way," I said, "thanks for looking at Ernie's cards as much as he did at yours. I wasn't looking forward to cutting his lawn all summer."

"Robert looked at Ernie's cards?" Mike echoed.

"Every single one that he dealt," I said with a nod. "Why don't you explain, Robert?"

Robert grinned. It was no longer a tight smile. It stretched from ear to ear.

"Feel the bottom of this card," he told Mike.

"Bumps," Mike said after a second.

"Braille," Robert corrected. "The special language that lets blind people read by feel."

Mike slowly understood, then roared with laughter.

"Yup," Robert said when Mike finally got his breath back. "Ernie thought he was pretty smart looking at my cards. But lots of times the guys who can use their eyes forget there's other ways to look at the world. So it didn't even occur to him that I could *feel* and recognize every card I dealt him. And after years of practice on mind maps, my memory's a lot better than his. He didn't have a chance."

Robert turned to me. "I will admit, though, I'm not going to be good at what comes next."

He reached out and grabbed and held my elbow with one hand, then pushed my open hand straight up in the air with the other. I waited, glad Robert couldn't see my puzzled look.

In a quick motion he slapped my palm with his free hand. Then he held his palm high for me.

"Give me five, pal," he said to me. "Give me five."

THE TROUBLE OF LIFE:
Thoughts on *Blindsided*

Life is difficult.

"This is a great truth, one of the greatest truths. It is a great truth because once we see, truly see, this truth, we rise above it.

"Once we truly know that life is difficult—once we truly understand and accept it—then life is no longer difficult. Because once it is accepted, the fact that life is difficult no longer matters."

If, like me, you prefer fast-paced books and movies with car chases, shooting, and pretty women, you may have raced through those first five sentences above, written by M. Scott Peck, M.D., in his book *The Road Less Traveled*.

I think I can promise, however, that if you understand and remember those five sentences, you will be granted a tremendous freedom.

First of all, what do those five sentences have to do with *Blindsided*?

Nothing.

And everything.

Nothing? Because *Blindsided* is a story about dealing with a handicap. Robert Johnson says, "I *am* a person, you know. Not an object of pity," and later he says, "The guys who can use their eyes forget there are other ways to look at the world." I was hoping, as a writer, that we'd see how easy it is to make the mistake of presuming a handicap makes someone a lesser person.

Nothing? Because when I first wrote *Blindsided*, I thought I was merely writing about that mistaken presumption.

Yet, much later, I read those five sentences and within the same week had a conversation with my father about changing the spark plugs in a boat's twin motors. And in one single sharp second during that conversation, the truth of those five sentences dawned on me—with the same breathtaking suddenness of the sun breaking through thunderclouds. Then I realized how much those words have to do with Robert Johnson and *Blindsided*.

Unfortunately, there is little exciting to relate about the spark plugs and the boat motor. No fire belowdecks. No story about being stranded miles away from shore in a storm with stalled motors.

Instead, I was with a friend who had happened to buy some bad gasoline, fuel that was contaminated with water. When water—instead of pure gasoline—reached the engine, the motors quit. But we were docked at the time, and fixing this problem was simply a matter of replacing the fuel filter and cleaning the spark plugs.

I thought of the first car I owned—the ugliest and slowest car in town, a 1965 Plymouth Valiant affectionately named *Killer*—and remembered how easy it had been to remove the spark plugs. Open the hood, pull the spark plug wires, reach over and crank the wrench.

Simple. So I volunteered to work on the boat motors.

Once the covers above the motors had been removed, however, I discovered that changing the spark plugs would not be easy. Not these boat motors.

The motors were set side by side below the rear deck. Even with the covers removed, they were still in near darkness. To reach these motors meant kneeling in a crawl space barely higher and wider than the motors themselves and groping blindly around the monstrous blocks of metal. Ankle-high oily water sloshed over my feet beneath the engines. The boat rocked. And there was no way to reach the spark plugs or even the spark plug wires without highly specialized equipment and backbreaking hours of effort.

Thus, barely minutes after volunteering to change the spark plugs, I resigned in total frustration.

I thought that my father, an automotive mechanic, would find my tale amusing. So I told him about it.

He merely smiled at my ignorance.

"Come on, Dad," I said. "Confess. It would drive you nuts to have to work on boats instead of cars."

His smile remained, and he disagreed with a shake of his head.

I snorted disbelief. "No way, Dad. You can change the spark plugs in a car in twenty minutes. It'd take you hours to do the same thing with the boat motor."

"That's true," he said. "But with the boat motor, I'd expect it to take three hours. Why would I be upset when I know it's supposed to take that long?"

And that's when it hit me.

Expectations.

I would appreciate it if you read Dr. Peck's five sentences again. Slowly.

Expectations.

If you expect it to be cold, and you dress warmly, it's no big deal. But if you go to Hawaii and have to shiver on the beach during a snowstorm, you'd be extremely disappointed.

If you plan on a two-mile hike and are still walking twelve miles later, you'll be disappointed. And so forth.

If you expect life to be a breeze, if you think life should be easy, then you will be forever disappointed, because *life is difficult.* Always.

When you finally accept that life will always be difficult—that when no sooner have you overcome one hurdle then you will be faced with another—it no long matters that life is difficult; it no longer frustrates you. You simply begin to overcome the next hurdle, with gratitude for any rest between.

Are you disappointed that you won't graduate from high school right after passing the sixth grade? Of course not. The sixth grade is one hurdle. You fully know there will be the hurdles of all those grades between.

For some, passing a grade is not a high nor difficult hurdle. Studying and memorization comes easily. Their problems lie elsewhere; many "brains" I knew wanted very badly to be good in school sports.

Life is difficult. Everyone has their own hurdles.

In *Blindsided*, Robert Johnson lives every minute of his life with one of the greatest hurdles you might imagine. He is blind. Yet he accepts the disadvantage and calmly works around it with his mind maps.

And that's why I think *Blindsided* has so much to do with Dr. Peck's five sentences.

On the surface, and when I first wrote it, I thought the story was about *us* making peace with Robert Johnson's handicap. Now I realize that, even before I could write the story, it was Robert Johnson who had to make peace with his handicap first, just as we all must make peace with the difficulties in our own lives.

It's a very practical message, the one from Dr. Scott Peck. Life is difficult, and once we accept it, we rise above the difficulties.

This is a story about instinct. Actually, two instincts. One that belonged to a middle-aged man in a wheelchair, who was known as Crazy Carl. And one that belonged to my six-year-old brother, Joel Kidd.

From the start, all I can tell you about instinct is that I have no idea how it works. And there wasn't much use asking Joel. He would just shrug. He's like a ghost, coming and going as quietly as smoke and disappearing like that same smoke whenever he's finished whatever he just did to scare you into a heart attack.

But somehow Joel knew.

And somehow Crazy Carl knew, too.

It started the day that my friend Mike challenged me to a Batman kite fight on Leighton Hill, the highest place in Jamesville, with hardly any trees. Perfect for kite flying in the summer when the wind was blowing. Perfect for sledding in the winter.

"Ricky, I'll tear you to shreds," he sneered.

"Actually," Ralphy broke in, "correctly speaking, you'll tear Ricky's kite to shreds, not *him*."

"Whatever, Einstein. His kite won't last more than twelve seconds in the air."

I grinned. Mike's got red hair that makes him do dumb

things, like thinking he can beat me in a kite fight. Ralphy's skinny and clumsy until you put him in front of a computer. Between the two of them, life is usually interesting. And Mike was right. A kite fight would be a great way to pass a Saturday afternoon, especially with our new Batman kites, which would swoop in every breeze.

"Mike, you're on. Consider your kite doomed. I'll meet you at the hill."

Naturally, I forgot to count on Joel.

He has no sense of property ownership. He does, however, have a great sense for finding any of my things that look fun. Like my kite. Which was missing.

"Moooommmmm!" I hollered from my bedroom. "Will you donate Joel to an adoption agency?"

She told me to quit yelling.

By the time I found Joel on a quiet side street nearby, it was much too late. Too late to meet Mike. Too late to ever use my kite again.

His attempts to fly it would have been funny, except it was my brother and my kite.

The little pest had tied his teddy bear to the string just below the kite. His determination was so amazing, I could only stand and stare for the first five minutes.

This is how it worked. Joel patiently propped the kite up. Then he carefully backed away from it and kept the string tight. When he had enough string out, he started to run, his tiny legs churning like pistons.

For someone smart enough to be patient, he sure was slow. Anybody else would have figured out after one or two runs that the teddy bear was much too heavy for the kite to make it into the air.

Not Joel. As I watched, he made five attempts. I knew he had made many more before I had arrived because of one small clue. My kite was torn to shreds from dragging along the asphalt.

I didn't have the heart to yell. Instead, after watching for that long, I simply walked up and said, "How much money do you have in your piggy bank? Enough to buy a new kite?"

Joel knew I was joking. He grinned. "Can you make teddy fly?"

I groaned. "Not when I'm busy skinning you alive. Come on, let's go home."

When I turned around, there he was. Crazy Carl. Blocking the middle of the street with his wheelchair. Scraggy hair, dark bags under his eyes, gray in his beard, torn shirt, and useless legs. I'd forgotten he lived two houses down.

He ignored me. "You want that teddy bear to fly, kid."

It wasn't a question.

Joel nodded eagerly.

"Be here tomorrow at two," Crazy Carl grunted. Then he finally looked at me. "You too. I'll need help getting up Leighton Hill."

He didn't wait for an answer. Just scowled and turned his chair to slowly and quietly wheel his way back to his house.

By the time we made it back the next day, I had a good idea why Crazy Carl was named Crazy Carl. And why he was helping Joel fly his teddy bear.

Dad had explained it at suppertime the night before. "Let him take Joel kite flying. It'll do Carl some good. The poor man hates the world because of the way he ended up in a wheelchair."

Mom had raised her eyebrows. "That might be a snap judgment."

Dad only smiled sadly. "Not really. We went to high school together. All he wanted was to be a jet pilot. He had his chance in the Gulf War and flew as many missions as anybody in his squadron. He figured he would never get hurt in the air. He was right. It was on the ground he broke his back. A freak accident in a jeep that was bringing him to the airfield one day."

"He's not crazy?" I asked.

"Only bitter, son. Last time I spoke to him was ten years ago. He hated God then, he told me, and always would. He stays away from everybody, he's so full of hate. Joel must have really touched his heart to get him to come out of the house."

So the next day I didn't ask Crazy Carl about flying or anything like that. He didn't seem friendly. In fact, he only grunted when Joel gave him two colored Sunday School cards as presents.

"Leighton Hill, kid," Crazy Carl barked at me when we arrived. A kite twice as wide as his wheelchair filled his lap.

I pushed him there to the top of the hill in silence. Joel walked beside him during the ten minutes it took.

"Leave me with sport here," he barked again. "Come back in an hour."

That's all he ever said to me every Sunday for the next few months when I brought Joel over. Those three sentences. "Leighton Hill, kid." "Leave me with sport here." "Come back in an hour."

What he and Joel talked about during those hours is a mystery to me. They'd have that huge kite in the air whenever I returned, with Joel's teddy bear flying high above them. Only once or twice on my return I caught Crazy Carl's gentle smile as he watched Joel grinning happily upward at his teddy bear. Once I caught him looking at those two colored Sunday School cards from Joel; it surprised me that he still kept them. Mostly, though, whenever I arrived, I seemed to break into their magic world.

Where the instinct comes in makes me believe what Dad told me later about it. Of course, when he told me, it was at a time when all of us were ready to believe that explanation.

You see, the last time that Crazy Carl went flying with Joel and his teddy bear, he finally spoke more than his two hilltop sentences.

The wind was blowing nicely, and Carl's voice seemed a little softer. "Take the kid back with you," he said quietly. "He's already agreed to let the teddy bear stay with me."

That was something. It usually takes skilled deception to pry Joel from the teddy bear.

"And take your time coming back," Crazy Carl said.

As I was turning and Crazy Carl was lifting the kite from his lap, I glimpsed both of Joel's Sunday School cards.

Each card is now high in my closet where I'm sure they'll never get lost. They were the kind with verses printed on and a drawing for the kids to color. One had Joel's scrawl all over it. "Jesus loves you, Cawrell," it said in orange crayon. The other card had a drawing of someone flying a kite—colored in yellow and purple and green and Joel hadn't stayed inside the lines anywhere—with the verse below it from Second Corinthians that read, "Now the Lord is the Spirit, and where the Spirit of the Lord is, there is freedom."

How did Joel know to give him those cards? And how did Joel know it would be the last time Crazy Carl would ever take him kite flying?

I can't answer. You see, when we walked back up the hill, Joel wasn't surprised to see Crazy Carl slumped over in the wheelchair, a peaceful expression on his now still face, with the kite string tied to one wheel and the teddy bear on the ground where it had fallen. Joel didn't panic or become alarmed when I ran as hard as I could to find a doctor. He just waited beside the wheelchair and smiled at the doctor when he arrived at the top of the hill.

And how did Carl know which Sunday afternoon would be the day he could really fly and leave his wheelchair behind, along with the Bible they found in his jacket?

I can't answer that, either.

All I know is how Dad explained instinct to me at Crazy Carl's funeral. "It's God's way of protecting His creatures," he whispered as Mom placed flowers in front of the fresh grave.

The breeze around us quickened. It wasn't hard to guess what Joel was thinking as he watched the wind pluck petals loose and carry them into the blue above us.

FREEDOM OF THE SPIRIT:
Thoughts on *Crazy Carl*

I CONFESS THAT CRAZY CARL is not original to any of you who have read other books in the ACCIDENTAL DETECTIVES series. In fact, if you've read *Sunrise at the Mayan Temple*, you might be a bit disappointed with me right now. After all, the story *Crazy Carl* is almost identical to the first and last chapters of that book, with the difference that the name of the war vet in the wheelchair has been changed from Crazy Carl to Mad Eddie.

Not only is this short story reused material, then, but even before suggesting to my editor that we include it, I guessed I would have an extremely difficult time gathering any thoughts on its theme—freedom of the spirit.

So why use *Crazy Carl*?

Sheer unabashed immodesty.

Crazy Carl won a small award once, complete with certificate-suitable-for-framing and a small check. (It wasn't exactly a Pulitzer Prize, but hey, an award is an award, and I'll take it any way I can get it, especially since I'm usually happy just to have someone paste a couple of gold stars on anything I write.)

Naturally, since the day of receiving that award, I've been determined to get as much mileage out of it as possible. After all, *Crazy Carl* may well be my last award-winning story, and even though everybody—mostly just all of my relatives—who even knew it won an award probably forgot about the entire thing within twenty-four hours, *I* won't turn my back on its significance.

Thus, the short story *Crazy Carl* found new life as the opening chapter in *Sunrise at the Mayan Temple*. Thus, here it is again.

Aside from immodesty, there is another reason why *Crazy Carl* appears again. I think it's because what happens between Joel and the man in the wheelchair who found freedom is still a wonderful mystery to me.

The story began simply because Dick Broene, my friend and editor of *The Crusader* magazine, asked if I would write a story on the theme "freedom of the spirit."

I knew then as little about how that might happen in a story as I do now.

Freedom of the spirit.

I didn't dare tell my fears to Dick Broene. He might change his mind about having me write it. (And paying me for it.)

So I began, with no idea that Joel would meet Crazy Carl, and even less of an idea about what would happen between the two of them. All I knew was that it needed to be a story about someone finding freedom. Now, several years later, I still don't really know what happened between them.

That might sound stupid. Wasn't I the one to write the story? Yet, with this story, I seemed less a writer and more an observer.

I could clearly picture Crazy Carl when I first "met" him through Ricky. I wondered what it might be like to be him, and I thought I understood. He was in a wheelchair, while those around him could walk, run, dance. Here was a man I knew, very angry and bitter at how life had imprisoned him.

Then I tried seeing Joel through this man's eyes, a man who had just watched a six-year-old kid doggedly try to fly a kite. How could you not have a little warmth for a kid who refuses to give up? You could remain bitter and angry at the rest of the world, but with Joel, an innocent kid, you could relax, let your guard down.

At that point, Ricky and I were no longer part of the story. Joel and Crazy Carl—worlds apart—were going to be friends. They trusted each other. Ricky and I were only able to watch, from the sidelines.

Freedom of the spirit?

When I think about it now, Crazy Carl probably had a right to be angry at the way his body imprisoned him. Yet to some degree, all of us are imprisoned by our bodies. The strength, or lack of strength, of our muscles and bones place upon us definite physical limitations. Against our will, our bodies age. Against our will, we become sick. We cannot soar on the wind with the grace of a hawk. We cannot knife through water with the power of a shark. We are earthbound and relatively clumsy and frail creatures.

From that perspective, Crazy Carl was merely imprisoned in a small cell at the side of the jail yard, enviously watching through iron bars as everyone else played within the shadows of the prison walls.

If that is true, then, that we are all prisoners of our physical selves—death takes even the strongest, wealthiest, wisest, and most free of us—then the only freedom we can find is through freedom of the spirit. Faith takes our focus from what binds us here on earth and lifts our eyes to something much grander than our physical restrictions. On a practical level, I believe that the same faith gives us a truer perspective of our earthbound troubles. Nothing on earth, not even death, is so overwhelming that it can take away the freedom of our spirits. And with that understanding, troubles are much easier to face.

Crazy Carl made that discovery, of course, sometime between meeting Joel and his last time flying a kite on Leighton Hill. How and why is a mystery to me. I'm guessing part of it is because with Joel, Crazy Carl finally let himself be open to a friendship, and friendship was the first step in looking beyond himself. Perhaps once he'd looked a little beyond himself, he could begin to see how much more there was than his tiny, self-absorbed world of anger.

I'm sure Joel's Sunday School cards helped, too. Here's a hard-ened war vet, scornful of everything. Had anyone else but Joel delivered that message—Jesus loves you—Crazy Carl would have spit in disgust. But given with childlike innocence and scrawled in crayon, it was a message Crazy Carl was able to consider as he looked beyond his own world.

The rest of how Crazy Carl found freedom of the spirit?

It's a story about instincts, I guess. Actually, two instincts . . . and from the start, all I can tell you about instinct is that I have no idea how it works.